It was too late.

They were driving straight toward the bridge.

Ben swerved, but he couldn't shake the SUV tailing them. "Hold on!" he yelled as the SUV rammed into them, flipping their car. They skidded before landing on the guardrail, teetering precariously toward the river below.

Upside down and disoriented, Jordan was afraid to move. She was alive, but for how long?

"Do you see the notebook?" Jordan asked. "I dropped it when we crashed. We can't let it fall into the river."

She suddenly heard a ripping sound, and she saw a knife sawing through the airbag by her door. She couldn't see who had cut away the thin nylon fabric, but she heard a small laugh. "Don't worry. I'll take care of it." An arm reached inside and snatched the notebook. Then the man put his hand on the frame of the car and pushed. "I hope you can swim."

The metal groaned, and Ben and Jordan could hear it bending and straining against the pull of gravity. Suddenly, the car tilted even farther toward the water, and the metal whined once more before the car careened toward the river below.

Kathleen Tailer is a senior attorney II who works for the Supreme Court of Florida in the office of the state courts administrator. She graduated from Florida State University College of Law after earning her BA from the University of New Mexico. She and her husband have eight children, five of whom they adopted from the state of Florida. She enjoys photography and playing drums on the worship team at Calvary Chapel in Thomasville, Georgia.

Books by Kathleen Tailer

Love Inspired Suspense

Under the Marshal's Protection
The Reluctant Witness
Perilous Refuge
Quest for Justice
Undercover Jeopardy
Perilous Pursuit
Deadly Cover-Up

Visit the Author Profile page at Harlequin.com.

DEADLY COVER-UP

KATHLEEN TAILER

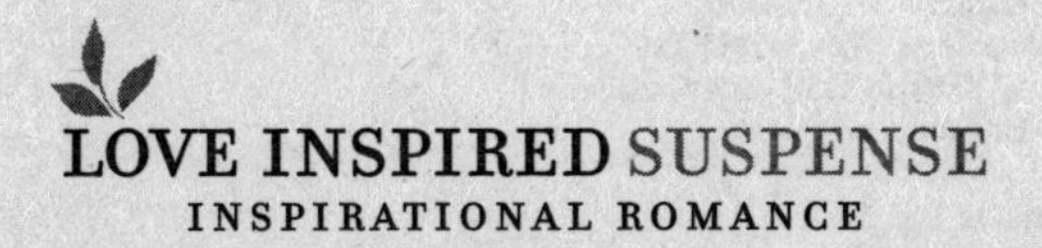

If you purchased this book without a cover you should be aware that this book is stolen property. It was reported as "unsold and destroyed" to the publisher, and neither the author nor the publisher has received any payment for this "stripped book."

Recycling programs for this product may not exist in your area.

ISBN-13: 978-1-335-40276-9

Deadly Cover-Up

Copyright © 2020 by Kathleen Tailer

All rights reserved. No part of this book may be used or reproduced in any manner whatsoever without written permission except in the case of brief quotations embodied in critical articles and reviews.

This is a work of fiction. Names, characters, places and incidents are either the product of the author's imagination or are used fictitiously. Any resemblance to actual persons, living or dead, businesses, companies, events or locales is entirely coincidental.

This edition published by arrangement with Harlequin Books S.A.

For questions and comments about the quality of this book, please contact us at CustomerService@Harlequin.com.

Love Inspired
22 Adelaide St. West, 40th Floor
Toronto, Ontario M5H 4E3, Canada
www.Harlequin.com

Printed in U.S.A.

I can do all things through Christ
which strengtheneth me.

—*Philippians* 4:13

For my wonderful and ever-growing family:
Jim, James, Bethany, Daniel, Keandra, Joshua O'Neal,
Jessica, Nathan, Joshua Evan, Anna and Megan.
And for all of my friends in Africa who are dedicated
to spreading the name of Jesus throughout the land.
May God bless all of you!

ONE

The man was still following her.

Jordan Kendrick pretended to read the ingredient list on a box of cereal but was still able to catch a quick glimpse of him in her peripheral vision as she turned the corner and went down a new aisle in the grocery store.

He'd already been watching her for over ten minutes, and the sight of him alone made her skin crawl and anxiety pump through her veins.

Dark hair and eyes. Light skin. He was wearing a University of Florida Gators T-shirt, but even so, she knew he was not a local. She would recognize those eyes anywhere. They were empty, and she noticed the same cold and vacant look from when he had tried to kill her in South Carolina. Jordan put a package of cheese and a couple of yogurts in her basket, then moved slowly to the next aisle. She glanced at him again, trying to appear nonchalant, even though adrenaline was coursing through her as the fear increased. The man had his own basket in his hand. He put a box or can of food in it every once in a while, but he was clearly just watching her and not shopping for his next meal.

Jordan hadn't wanted to go out today, but her pantries were bare, and she'd desperately needed to buy groceries. Living on the run was no picnic, and constantly watching her surroundings to make sure she was safe was beginning to take a toll on her. Dark circles had formed under Jordan's eyes, and she had lost several pounds, as the stress had eaten away at her stomach. Still, she had to eat something.

She couldn't figure out how the man had found her. She had been so careful, and she was bone weary from playing this cat and mouse game in the first place. Now she couldn't even go back to the small room she had rented. For all she knew, this man knew where she lived and had followed her when she'd left the building. Jordan knew he would stop at nothing until he had eliminated her from the face of the earth.

How was she going to survive this latest threat?

The man was wearing a thin jacket, even though it was over ninety degrees outside, and when he leaned forward to pick up an apple from the produce section, she got a glimpse of the pistol he had tucked into his waistband. He was there to kill her. She had no doubt about it. He was just biding his time, waiting for the right opportunity when there wouldn't be any witnesses to catch him in the act.

Jordan glanced up at the ceiling, noting where the cameras were located and hoping that at least one of them had recorded her pursuer's face. If she was going to lose her life, she at least wanted the man captured after the fact. Her colleagues had already been killed, yet to date, no one had been charged.

A moment of indecision held her frozen for a few moments as she contemplated her next move. She couldn't stand in the produce section forever, but she didn't know where else to go. She couldn't go into the bathroom at the back of the store. If she did, he would surely follow her in and kill her in the quiet of the stockroom where there were no other people or cameras. Her only hope was to stay in a populated area until she could slip away into the crowd. The only problem was, the store was slowly emptying and there were only a few customers left amongst the aisles. For all she knew, her pursuer might have disabled any cameras that existed before he had even entered the store, and he might try to kill her as soon as they were alone. She could approach someone that worked in the store, but how could they possibly protect her against a man with a gun? She hadn't seen a security guard anywhere, but even if one appeared, she doubted a part-timer would be able to really help. In fact, it would probably just put the guard's life at risk, as well. This man was a professional. He was a serious threat, and she really didn't want anyone else hurt because of her.

She had to get out of there. Now. But how?

She came to the end of her aisle that was close to the registers, and finally, an idea hit her. There was a large display of canned goods on the endcap. What she needed was a good distraction. She surreptitiously hit the bottom row with her foot, then scrambled out of the way as the entire tower of soup cans crashed to the ground. The noise was deafening, but it hardly registered as she dropped her basket and ran toward the exit as fast as her feet could carry her.

"Hey, lady, stop!" the cashier yelled as she passed, but Jordan was too scared to heed her instructions, or to even look behind her to see how close the assassin was. A wall of sticky humidity hit her as she burst outside under the Florida sunshine, and she could smell the summer rain that had just left a sheen of moisture everywhere she looked. She made it to the parking lot, then scrambled between a jeep and a large pickup truck and instantly bent down, trying to hide between the two vehicles. Her breathing was coming in gasps, and she leaned against the truck for a moment, trying to catch her breath. Thankfully, even though there were a few people walking around in the parking lot, nobody seemed to be paying any attention to her. She glanced back over her shoulder. It didn't look like anyone had follow her out of the store.

She glanced at the sky. It was about five or so in the evening, and it wasn't nearly dark enough outside to cover her escape, even with the passing storm clouds. She made a mental note to only shop when it was dark from now on…if she survived this attack in the first place.

She heard a couple arguing near their car, and another car drove into a nearby parking spot with the radio blaring. She crouched and moved both farther away from the Jeep and farther away from the store, using the various cars as cover for her getaway, hoping that the noise and the movements in the parking lot would distract her pursuer.

He found her, anyway.

The first bullet ripped into the rear fender of the car that she had been leaning against, only inches from her cheek. It left a jagged hole in the metal, as did his second shot that hit the vehicle a scant inch from the first. The impacts made very little noise, but she felt both bullets whiz by her head. Her pursuer must be using a silencer, she thought fleetingly. She ducked instantly, right as the third bullet hit the side door panel of the car about eight inches higher. She let out a yelp and hit the ground, ignoring the small wet pebbles and dirt that were embedding themselves in her skin. Quickly, she rolled under a nearby truck, got back on her feet and started running out of the parking lot and toward the busy street beyond, using the parked cars and trucks as cover the best she could. She dared not look behind her. She was sure she would freeze like a statue if she turned and actually saw how close the assassin was following. If she could just make it to the road and get across it, she might actually survive this encounter. There was a park and several small stores on the other side of the street, as well as groups of people walking and talking as they followed a sidewalk around a small lake. Others were walking pets and playing with small children at a large playground. Surely, she could hide amongst the people if she could just make it to the other side. If not, she was as good as dead.

Dear, God, she prayed silently, *please help me get away from this madman with the gun. Show me where to go.*

Pain suddenly sliced through her arm, and the impact

sent her to her knees and skidding against the pavement. Her breath was coming in gasps. She picked herself up as fast as she could, ignoring the blood that was dripping down her arm and the new scratches on her knees. Her bicep had gotten the worst of it, and the tender flesh felt like it was on fire. She crouched behind a car that was just pulling into the parking lot, using it the best she could for cover as it turned and drove toward the front of the store. She abandoned it after a few seconds and looked quickly into the road, then waved at the coming driver with her good arm as she stepped out into the traffic. She could see the man's eyes widen as he slammed on the brakes and saw his car skid to the left. The back started jackknifing but she kept moving, causing a car in the next lane to screech to a halt, as well. From there, everything seemed to happen in slow motion. She heard metal crunch as the car was hit from behind, but confusion and yelling ensued, giving her an opportunity to go into the third lane. This car's driver also slammed on the brakes, but she wasn't able to avoid the vehicle completely. It had been going in the opposite direction, and she rolled off the hood as it tried to stop without hitting her. Thankfully, Jordan could tell the car's impact would only leave her with some bruises, and her spike of adrenaline kept this new pain from barely even registering.

She kept running. The next lane was clear, and she darted into the city park, aiming to use one of the many live oaks for cover. She heard a sickening thud behind her and finally took a moment to stop and glance over her shoulder. Her pursuer had been struck by a black

Prius and was lying prone on the road. His gun had flown from his hand and was on the pavement a few feet from his outstretched fingers. Horns were honking, and several people had gotten out of their vehicles and were coming up to the man to check on him. They were so focused on the victim lying in the street that no one spoke to her or even glanced in her direction. She didn't wait to see what happened next. She turned and continued to run into the park, her good hand grasping her injured arm above the elbow where the bullet had hit.

She came upon a couple of teams playing softball in a sports field, and both had good-sized audiences cheering them on, despite the inclement weather. She turned right, avoiding the game and the people. Now that the man was no longer chasing her, she didn't want to be remembered by anyone along her path, and she imagined that a woman bleeding from a gunshot wound would definitely stick in a person's memory. Any Good Samaritan would also want to take her to the hospital, but that was simply too dangerous. Not only would that make it easier for enemies to find her, but the doctor would also report the incident to the police, and she already knew the police couldn't help her.

Where could she go now? How had the assassin found her? She didn't know where she had made a mistake, but she couldn't afford to make another one. Even if the man in the road died, there would be others.

What should she do?

She stopped running and leaned against another tree, trying to catch her breath. It was still coming in gasps, and she leaned over, her stomach retching. Surely, the man had died in the road. Even though he had been trying to kill her, she hadn't wanted him dead. She sank down farther against the base of the tree, finally ending up on the ground as she fought the nausea. Eventually, a semblance of normalcy returned, and her eyes closed for a moment as she considered her next move. Gingerly, she pulled her fingers away from her wounded arm, trying to assess the damage. The pain was intense, but it wasn't just her arm that was hurting. The fear that swept over her was almost debilitating. She couldn't stop the tears that suddenly began to flow down her cheeks. She had survived this latest encounter, but would she survive the next? What should she do? She was at the end of her rope.

She started to pray.

Ben Graham was so emotionally drained that he didn't feel like cooking, so he drove through his favorite fast-food chicken restaurant for a grilled-chicken sandwich, fries and a tall cup of lemonade and ate while he maneuvered through the streets. He parked in his driveway and headed inside his house, a small two-bedroom bungalow that was a few streets away from the beach. It wasn't fancy, but what his house lacked in style was made up for by its proximity to the ocean. He realized he could probably never afford beachfront property on his salary, but this small house's location made it possible for him to run on the beach nearly every morning before he headed to the office. During those early morning hours, there was rarely anyone near the water, so he enjoyed the peace and quiet, as well as many beautiful sunrises, as he watched the sun light up the Atlantic Ocean each day.

He made his way inside and dropped his dinner trash in the kitchen bin, then went into the living room and pulled his gun out of the holster and laid it on the end table. He wearily sat down on the couch, his thoughts in chaos. What a day this had been! He leaned back for a moment and closed his eyes, once again going over the arrest he had made earlier that afternoon while on duty as a deputy with the Jacksonville Sheriff's Office. The man had started off as a prescription drug abuser and had rapidly become a "frequent flyer." He had been arrested several times during the last year for illegal drug use, but he just couldn't break the habit. This time, he had been near death when they found him suffering from an overdose of heroin in a deserted alley. Knowing his history, they quickly administered Narcan, a drug that counteracted the effects of the opioid. The Narcan helped them revive him, and the man instantly started breathing normally again, once the medication had entered his system. Typically, Ben would have waited for the emergency response personnel to administer the restorative medicine, but there simply hadn't been time to wait. He wondered if the man would survive if he overdosed again. They had found him just in the nick of time, but if he didn't get clean, Ben didn't see much hope for his future. The man had a wife and two children, all who would grieve his death if he wasn't able to kick his horrible drug habit.

"Hello, Ben."

The voice behind him was soft, but he instantly recognized it, and it sent a shiver down his spine. Nevertheless, he immediately grabbed his pistol, turned and pointed it in the direction of the voice, his eyes quickly focusing on the form who stood a few feet away from his couch. Jordan Kendrick, his fiancée, was dead. She couldn't be in his house or standing in his living room.

It couldn't really be her.

He was going crazy. That was it. Dead people didn't suddenly reappear. Yet, the woman he had loved had suddenly materialized in front of him, right in his living room. And she was not an apparition. So, what was going on? He looked cautiously around his living room, wondering if anyone else was going to pop out of the woodwork. Was somebody playing some sort of sick trick on him?

His gaze returned to the woman, and he took a moment to study her. Jordan's hair had been darker. This woman was a blond and thinner. Yet, the lady in front of him looked remarkably like his fiancée, who had died tragically in a boating accident a little over nine months ago. Sure, her hair was different, and his fiancée had always worn trendy wire-rimmed glasses, but this woman could be wearing contacts, and a box of hair dye was available just about anywhere for under ten bucks.

Still, it couldn't be her. His mind told him what his heart refused to accept—Jordan Kendrick was dead. He had edited the obituary himself, attended the funeral and helped her parents sort through her belongings and clean out her apartment. She was gone forever. Wishful thinking couldn't bring someone back, even if they had been deeply loved. So, who was this woman, and why was she in his house?

"Ben, it's me. Jordan." Her voice was barely above a whisper.

"Jordan Kendrick is dead," he responded, with a touch of menace in his tone. "Who are you?"

TWO

"It's me, Ben. Really."

Her voice was the same. Or maybe that was foolish dreaming on his part, as well. Jordan Kendrick had been the love of his life, and even though he knew she was dead and gone, his heart still fluttered at the possibility of her still being alive. He would give anything to hold her one last time. They had never actually found her body in the ocean, although the boat she'd been sailing in had capsized about thirty miles offshore. There had been no evidence of foul play, either, and the authorities had done a search-and-rescue operation for five days before calling it quits and declaring her dead.

He slowly stood, keeping his gun trained on her midriff. "It can't be. Jordan Kendrick was killed in a boating accident nine months ago." Still, a large part of him wanted this to be Jordan so badly. She had been so vibrant, so full of life. There was a giant hole in his heart ever since her death—one that he didn't feel like he could ever fill again. Seeing someone that looked like her brought a new flash of pain that swept over him from head to toe, reminding him of his loss.

Even though Jordan had been gone for nine months, Ben was still grieving. Maybe it was easier for those left behind when there was a body to mourn and bury. Maybe if he'd seen the damaged boat in person or been with her when she had gone overboard, he would have been able to get past the heartache that still seemed to overwhelm him from time to time in the oddest places. Even last week, he had been walking down the aisle at the supermarket and had been suddenly overcome with a sense of loss, just at the sight of her favorite sweet in the candy aisle. Grief was funny that way. Just when he thought he had a handle on it, some unexpected memory would trigger the pain and sorrow all over again. He hoped that time would erase those feelings, or at least lessen them so they wouldn't be so intense, but he was still overcome at times.

Now, all of those feelings were back in full force and hitting him all at once.

"It's really me, Ben," the woman said softly, her voice breaking into his reverie. "I promise. Remember how we used to picnic on the beach and you used to go diving for spiny lobster while I stayed on shore, reading the latest romance novel?"

He shook his head. "Plenty of people do that."

"Do plenty of people stop in the middle of grabbing lobsters to arrest a guy for taking fourteen lobsters over the limit?"

Her question astounded him. Few people knew about that arrest. He usually didn't bother with marine violations since the Fish and Wildlife Conservation Commission or the coast guard kept most folks in compliance with the law, but that particular lobster violation had really bothered him, so he had made the stop. The perpetrator had turned out to be a high-powered congressman from New York State with plenty of pull—so much so that he had managed to keep the arrest out of the news. The politician had paid a large fine and quietly returned to his home state.

Ben raised an eyebrow as his stomach did a flip-flop. Could it be true? Was Jordan Kendrick still alive? Part of him wanted to believe it, yet he had so many questions, and pain inundated him from head to toe. If she had been alive all this time, why hadn't she contacted him? Had Jordan or someone else faked her death? Why would she do it? What frightful necessity would have driven her to such lengths?

Was the love they'd shared real or just a fallacy?

He watched her shift from one foot to another. She was uncomfortable, too. When she spoke, her voice trembled. "Remember when I cooked those ribs on the grill, and I completely burned them up? Flames were shooting out of the grill, and you rushed out and drenched the charcoal, convinced I was about to burn your house down. By the time we got the mess cleaned up, the rest of the food was also ruined. We ended up going out to eat at that barbeque place you like so much—Robbie's, the restaurant on Pine Street down in Palm Valley. We were nearly starving by the time we arrived, and I'd never seen you eat so much. Then we went back to my place and watched old black-and-white movies until midnight. Despite the fire, it turned out to be one fantastic evening."

It was her.

Nobody else would know those details. Jordan was alive! Ben felt his heartbeat accelerate, and the sound seemed to be roaring in his ears. He stood there motionless for several seconds as the fact that she hadn't died nine months ago washed over him. "Where have you been? How can this be true?" He took a step forward.

She took a step back and put up her hands. "I'm alone, I promise. And unarmed. Can you put that gun down?"

Ben quickly engaged the safety and laid the weapon on the table. He wanted to reach for her and pull her into his arms, but he instantly sensed that she wouldn't welcome his embrace. He wasn't even sure if she would allow his touch. She seemed poised to run and was acting like a terrified rabbit being chased through a forest. Her eyes were wide, and he noticed blood on her arm and shirt. How had she gotten injured? His heart continued to beat frantically against his chest, and he took another step toward her.

She jerked and took a step back. Her eyes darted around the room, apparently seeking a quick retreat, and her features showed her insecurity and doubt. Her hands fisted and unfisted as if she couldn't quite stand still. Was she going to bolt, now that she had finally approached him?

He sensed her hesitance and fear, and he put up his hands in a motion of surrender. When he spoke, he kept his voice soft, almost like a whisper. "Is it really you?" he asked again, still not quite believing it.

"Yeah, it's me. I promise."

Even though she wouldn't let him touch her, his eyes

consumed her. She had changed so much. A wariness covered her face that worried him, and fine lines of stress were clearly visible around her eyes and mouth. The weight loss made her cheekbones more prominent, but her lips were still full and elegant. Her clothes were stained and torn, and her hands had started shaking. He could see that her nails were shredded, and she had several scrapes on her hands and knees. Still, she was the most beautiful woman he had ever seen. His heart fluttered, and he slowly dropped his hands.

"How are you alive?" he whispered.

"It's a long story."

A host of emotions played across his chest. Why had she deceived him? And why had she waited nine months before contacting him? Anger bubbled to the surface before he could stop it. "A long story? Really? I spoke at your funeral nine months ago and now you appear out of nowhere and say hello like we were passing acquaintances? I thought you were dead!"

She backed even farther away from him until she was almost in the corner, and he instantly regretted letting the anger escape. He might be justified in his ire, but Jordan had always been a caring and loving woman. There had to be a good reason for what she'd done. He needed to give her the benefit of the doubt, at least until he knew what had happened and she'd had a chance to explain.

She bit her bottom lip, a motion that was pure Jordan and so familiar to him. His whole body felt like it was on the verge of exploding. How was she here, standing in front of him? His brain still couldn't seem to comprehend it. Yet, here she was, living and breathing right in his living room, and apparently scared to death about something or someone by the way she was acting. He tried again, softening his voice. "I'm sorry. I don't mean to yell. This is just a bit hard for me to process." He rubbed the back of his neck in frustration and lowered his voice even further. He wanted to touch her so badly. "How?" he stammered. "How are you here? How are you alive?"

She glanced around the room as if verifying the exits, and he could see her wide blue eyes. Only they weren't blue—they were brown now. She was definitely wearing contacts. But her high thin eyebrows and perky nose hadn't changed, and the sprinkle of freckles was still scattered across her face. However, there were dark splashes under her eyes that looked stress-induced, and her skin had lost its healthy tone. He took another step forward, and finally she didn't retreat as he advanced. He moved slowly, purposefully, and reached over and lightly touched her face with the pads of his fingers. This time, she didn't back away. Soft skin met his trembling fingertips. Yes, she was definitely real. And she smelled like Jordan—a sweet mixture of lavender and mint. His heart was beating so hard it felt like a bass drum in his chest. Could this really be happening? Could the love of his life really still be alive and standing before him?

Jordan covered his large hand with her smaller one and squeezed it, then glanced around nervously, again making sure they were alone and nobody had followed her. She knew it would be hard on Ben if she decided to approach him, and now she had to give him time to accept it. Still, she wasn't happy about bringing him into her problems, and doing so was causing her a great deal of angst. Only nine short months ago, they had been planning their wedding. Now she was on the run and her life was in danger, and she had just put Ben's life in danger as well by coming back into his life. It didn't sit well with her, but she had run out of options.

Seeing Ben again did funny things to her insides. She still loved him, and she missed him terribly. Losing him had been her biggest regret when the US Marshals had helped her fake her death and enter the witness protection program. She had joined in the first place to protect him, and she still thought she had made the right decision at the time. Ben had believed she was gone forever, but that had been a small price to pay to keep him safe. Yet now, everything had changed. She was still being hunted, and she had no doubt that even though the man that had chased her at the grocery store had died, there would be others not far behind. The marshals who had promised to protect her had failed miserably, and she was out of options. She'd left the safe house in South Carolina and returned to Jacksonville, Florida, where all of her problems had originated in the first place. She'd purposefully made the choice to come home so she could continue investigating her case, but the decision to return still caused knots in her insides. She didn't want to put Ben in danger again, but the threat against her was very real and growing exponentially, and she didn't know what else to do.

Jordan ran her hands up and down her arms in a half-hearted motion of comfort. She was scared, even more so now than nine months ago when this all began. She was a scientist, not a law enforcement officer. The foe she faced was malevolent and powerful. Could a lone sheriff's deputy really do anything to stop the wave of terror that was filling her life? She bit her bottom lip, trying to calm the battle that was raging within her. Ben was good at his job—very good. She had seen him accomplish amazing things within his unit and help a lot of people. They had dated for over a year, and she felt like she had really gotten to know him during that time. Ben was amazing. He was caring and honest. He was the love of her life, and in her book, the most attractive man on the planet. But he was only one man. And she didn't want him dead.

She was assailed by doubts. She had made a mistake. She should never have come to Ben's house today. She needed to face these problems on her own—not drag Ben into them with her. She was strong and capable, and she just needed more time to think everything through. Her eyes darted to the door, and she turned, ready to run.

"Don't go," Ben said firmly.

Jordan turned back and glanced into his eyes. She saw a host of emotions all swimming together in those brown depths, but confusion and caring trumped them all. The confidence she saw was almost her undoing. She was completely terrified and didn't know where else to turn. And she was fooling herself. She wasn't able to do this on her own. She hadn't seen anyone following her to his house, but she still didn't feel comfortable staying out in the open for very long. She needed to disappear, but since WITSEC was no longer a possibility, she definitely needed Ben's help. She had no choice. She had nowhere else to go.

Would Ben help her? She refused to guess at his feelings. His expression alone showed how truly overwhelmed he was by her appearance. Still, he had loved her once. But she had lost the ability to read him or tell what he was thinking. She hoped he would help, but she wasn't banking on his cooperation.

She let out a breath. "I don't know if we can talk here. It might not be safe." She stepped back, glanced out the living room window, then pulled the curtains closed so that no one could see in.

He raised his eyebrows. "What are you talking about?"

"My life is in danger, Ben. That's why I disappeared in the first place. I've been in the federal witness protection program ever since the boating accident."

He shook his head, surprise splashed across his features. "WITSEC? Why? I don't understand. I had no idea. I mean, I know you were having some problems at the lab, but nothing that was so bad it would force you into hiding..."

"They'll come after you, too, if they see us together. I... I didn't want to put you in danger." She looked back at his face, which had been so dear to her. It was filled with confusion and hurt. His expression and her internal battles nearly overwhelmed her with the desire to throw herself into his arms and seek refuge in his embrace. She had always felt safe and secure around Ben. He was a big bear of a man, with broad shoulders and an athletic build that made it seem like he could handle whatever the world threw at him.

Yet, once again, doubts assailed her. This was wrong. She should have found a different way. Whether he could handle it or not, she had no right to drag him into the middle of her problems. She still had a little money left. Perhaps the solution was simply leaving Florida altogether and never coming back. If she left now, her case would never be resolved, but at least she would still have her life.

She paced a bit, still unsure.

Up until now, she'd always been good at solving her own difficulties. She would just have to do it once more. She was smart and creative. She'd graduated at the top of her class for her bachelor's degree and had earned the top marks for her master's and doctorate degrees, as well. Yet, after nine months, she was no closer to fixing her problems than she had been on that fateful day when she had gone into WITSEC in the first place. Being smart didn't make her invincible. And she needed help. Desperately.

What should she do? The question ate at her and made her stomach twist in knots. As her emotions played tug-of-war, she met Ben's eyes once more, but the pain and confusion she saw in his eyes was her undoing. "I shouldn't be here. This was a mistake—a big one," she murmured. Her eyes darted around the room one last time, and she started heading toward the back door.

THREE

Ben moved to block her, his voice firm. "No, this wasn't a mistake. Now that I know you're really alive, if you run, I'll find you. That's a promise. But you can save me the trouble. Tell me what's going on, Jordie. Let me in."

"I can't." Jordan took a few more steps but he grasped her arm and stopped her. Although he wasn't holding her tightly, she cried out at his touch. Without realizing it, his hand was only a few inches from her wound.

He loosened his grip but didn't let go completely and moved closer so he could examine her arm. "Good grief! You've been shot!" He shifted his hold but still didn't release her and gently led her back toward his bathroom. She blew out a frustrated breath, but finally gave in to his tender urging. He flipped on the light, then reached under the sink and pulled out a first aid kit. "We need to get you to a hospital," he said softly, caring in his voice.

"No. I won't go."

"That's crazy!" he said vehemently, yet still his voice was hushed. "You need medical attention."

"They require proof of identity and money, both of which I don't have."

"I'll pay," Ben responded quickly. More doubt filled her mind. Her enemies would definitely find her and kill her if she walked through the doors of a hospital. Hospitals also kept records and were forced to report bullet wounds. Sure, they had rules about confidentiality, but those rules couldn't protect her. Her adversary was just too powerful. She glanced nervously around the small bathroom. She should leave. Now. Somehow, she would figure a way out of this herself. "No," she said forcefully. "I'm not going to any hospital. I'll take care of it. I really am sorry I bothered you." She tried to keep the desperation from her voice, but she heard it quaver.

Ben quickly raised his hands in mock surrender. "Okay, Jordan. You win. We'll do it your way." He took a step forward as if he was going to take her in his arms, but she stiffened, and her reaction stopped him. She wouldn't meet his eye, so he just stood there, ostensibly waiting for her to acknowledge him. Finally, he touched her chin and gently lifted it until their eyes met.

She would not cry in front of him, she thought fiercely, even though she was suddenly lost in the depths of his chocolate-brown eyes. The caring and concern she saw reflected there was nearly her undoing.

Somehow, he seemed to understand that now wasn't the time to push for answers. He turned his focus to her arm, got some hydrogen peroxide and cotton balls and lightly started cleaning her wound. He continued in silence for several minutes, his touch comforting. When he finally did speak, his voice was calm and soft, almost soothing.

"So, it looks like the bullet went straight through. You've got an entrance wound here, and an exit wound here." He touched her skin gently, showing her. "As far as bullet wounds go, this is a pretty simple one that looks like it just did some basic muscle damage. It missed the bone completely. It's gonna hurt for a while, but you'll heal up in a few weeks or so." He put some antibiotic on both wounds, then pulled the skin closed with butterfly bandages. "You should still get it checked by a medical professional. I'm no doctor. If you get stitches, the scar won't be as bad, but you'd have to get them pretty soon." She said nothing, not wanting to argue, and thankfully he let the subject drop.

He finished by wrapping gauze around her arm and gently taping the end. Then he cleaned and bandaged her scraped knees and hands, frowning at the bruises he saw on her legs. Finally, he handed her a few extra bandages and the small tube of antibiotic for later, and she pocketed them. "I've got some pain reliever in the kitchen. How about we go get some for you?"

She nodded, finally feeling comfortable enough to relax a bit under Ben's ministrations. Her arm really did hurt, but it was the least of her worries. The stress and fear that she had been carrying for the last several months suddenly overcame her, and all she wanted to do was crawl into a hole and disappear. At least she was somewhat safe for the moment and Ben was nearby. She let him lead her into the kitchen, where he gave her some ibuprofen and a glass of water.

"You need to eat something when you take that medicine so it won't hurt your stomach. What can I fix you?"

His tone was kind, and his offer sincere, but she didn't feel hungry. What she felt was tired. Her lack of sleep and constant vigilance were catching up to her. Still, she recognized the truth in his words and didn't want to deal with a stomachache on top of everything else.

"Maybe just something simple. Do you have any crackers and peanut butter? I know how much you love that snack."

He nodded and pulled out a sleeve of wheat crackers, a knife and a half-eaten jar of creamy peanut butter. Ben could put peanut butter on anything and ate it by the spoonful when they had been dating. Those were fond memories. He liked the natural variety that didn't have any added ingredients but the peanuts themselves, and she had ditched her old brand and started buying the same jar, simply to have some on hand whenever he was around. After a few months, she had learned to love it almost as much as he did.

She slathered a couple of crackers in the sticky stuff and looked up as she took her first bite. He was still watching her every move, but his eyes held some undefinable emotion that she couldn't quite pin down. There was a time when she had been able to read him like a book, but that was before she had led him on such an emotional roller coaster. She wondered fleetingly if he could ever forgive her for her actions. She took another bite, pushing that thought aside for now. At this point, survival had to come first. Everything else had to wait.

"You're about to fall down with exhaustion, Jordan. You're safe here. I'll make sure of it. Why don't you sleep for a while? We can talk after you've had a chance to rest." He drew his lips into a thin line. "You can have the guest bedroom. The sheets are clean. I promise."

She bit her bottom lip again as she considered his offer, then finished off her crackers. She couldn't go on much longer without sleep, and she really had nowhere else to go. "I do need some sleep, Ben, but you have to promise me you won't tell anyone that I'm here. I've already put you in danger just by coming to your house. I don't want to put anybody else's life in jeopardy, too."

Ben stood up a little straighter. "I am a law enforcement officer, you know. I work with a good bunch of deputies. Whatever you're facing, we can help…."

"No." She steeled her voice. "If you can't promise me, then I can't stay. Those are my terms. I feel guilty enough already for involving you."

He took a step back and put up his hands again. Apparently, he realized that arguing was futile, at least at this point. "Alright, Jordan. We're going to play by your rules. For now, that is, until you tell me what's going on and we talk it through."

"Thank you, Ben." She nodded her head, trying to keep the weariness at bay. "Sleep sounds good. I promise I'll explain everything as soon as I rest a bit." She was tempted to give him a kiss on the cheek but decided against it. She had hurt him terribly, and she no longer had the right to kiss him or even show him affection. For all she knew, he had moved on and was dating someone new. The last thing she wanted to do was cause a rift in any relationship he was pursuing on top of everything else. The idea of him with someone different was a painful one, however, and a wave of jealousy swept over her that she hadn't expected. She was so tired. Every emotion she was feeling was amplified by ten.

She needed rest. She'd been to his house several times when they were dating, so she knew the layout. She gave him one last smile, then padded back to the bedroom he'd offered and was asleep within minutes of her head touching the pillow.

Ben stood in the doorway, watching Jordan sleep. He couldn't believe how drastically his life had changed in the last few hours. She was alive! Yet, she was a shadow of her former self and filled with fear and apprehension. It hurt his heart to see the condition she was in, and the way she kept pushing him away every time he tried to reach out. She was obviously terrified of something or someone, and his first instinct had been to call on his team at the Sheriff's Office. But he hadn't. He wanted to respect her wishes, at least for now, until he truly understood whatever danger she was facing. There would be plenty of time to call later after they had a long talk and she explained everything. Besides, Jordan was very independent and always tried to solve her own problems. Her enemy must be powerful indeed, if she had gone so far as to leave the safety of WITSEC and reach out to him for help. He knew instinctively that if he broke his word and called his team before she was ready, he would break the tenuous connection they currently had between them, and that was the last thing he wanted.

Ben took a deep breath and stretched, trying to ease some of the tension that had settled across his shoulder blades. He considered going to bed himself, even though it was a tad early, but he didn't think he could sleep, knowing Jordan was alive and in his house. There were too many unanswered questions spinning around in his mind. Who had shot her? And what if she woke up, had second thoughts and decided to disappear again? She'd already tried to leave a couple of times during their short conversation. He just couldn't allow that to happen—not after he had just gotten her back. He'd meant what he'd said, too—now that he knew she was alive, if she disappeared on him again, he wouldn't stop looking until he found her.

The solution was simple. He turned on the light in his hallway, grabbed the latest Lee Child book that he was reading and his sidearm, and sank down onto the floor, right outside her door. He leaned his head back against the doorjamb and blew out a breath. There was only one way for someone to hurt Jordan on his watch, and that would be by crawling over his body. There was a bedroom window, but it was tightly locked, and he was a light sleeper. If he did manage to snooze, he would definitely wake up if someone tried to open the window or sneak by him. Since she was so scared of something or someone, maybe when she woke up she would feel more at ease knowing that he was here, right outside the doorway with his weapon, protecting her.

Dear, God, help me know how to help Jordan. Please

let her get the rest she needs and help her to trust me so I can do my best to get her out of whatever mess she's in. Thank you for bringing her back to me. Amen.

The prayer was short but heartfelt. His faith was strong. He knew God was faithful and would help them with whatever they were facing. He turned his head and let his eyes roam over Jordan's face, remembering every detail. She was still sleeping soundly. He felt like he could watch her sleep all night. As relieved as he was that she was alive and back in his life, he was also wondering how he could ever trust her again. He knew the WITSEC rules, but although she had mentioned some problems at work before her disappearance, she'd never given any indication that she was mixed up with something as dangerous as a federal crime that required witness protection. Why hadn't she told him? Had he ever really known her? He shifted. Even if they were able to solve whatever problems she was facing, it would be quite a while before he would be able to stop worrying that she was going to disappear without a trace a second time, just like she had nine months ago.

Ben closed his eyes for moment and took a breath. She must have been planning her disappearance for several days before her alleged death. He opened his eyes and rubbed them. How had he missed this? He'd thought he really knew her. If she had been facing something of that magnitude, he should have been able to tell.

He glanced at her again. Why has she reappeared now? And why had she disappeared in the first place? Part of him wanted to wake her up right now just so he could get the answers to the dozens of questions that were flying around in his head, but he held back. He knew she needed rest. He was just going to have to be patient and wait. He studied her face, peaceful in sleep, memorizing every detail.

Could he ever trust her again?

FOUR

Jordan awoke with a start. Where was she? She had been dreaming, but all she remembered was a sense of fear and desperation. The rest was a blur. She blinked the remnants away and took in her surroundings. The room was dark, yet the light from the hallway illuminated Ben's figure that was right outside the doorway. He was dozing, his chin near his chest, a novel with a bookmark sticking out still sitting by his right hand and his pistol only a few inches away. He looked terribly uncomfortable, yet peaceful at the same time. She rose up on her elbows, listening carefully, but she didn't hear any other noises except cicadas chirping outside and Ben's steady breathing. The clock on the bedside table said it was a little after midnight. Her stomach growled, reminding her just how long ago she had eaten those crackers and peanut butter, and how little she had eaten the day before.

"Sounds like you're hungry," Ben said softly.

She snapped her head in his direction and was surprised to see him move and adjust his position. Slowly, he turned and looked at her. She was amazed that he was awake, and he reminded her of a bear coming out of hibernation—powerful yet deceptively languid. Her stomach growled again, and she grimaced. "I haven't been eating regularly. I guess my body isn't too happy about it."

"Feel like talking, or would you like to eat something first?"

"Food can wait." She sat up. "Are you guarding the door so I don't leave while you're sleeping?"

He shrugged and turned so now he was partly in the room. "I'm keeping the bad guys out for you. I wanted to make sure you felt safe and got some of the rest you needed."

She wasn't sure that was the only reason, but she let his comment go, appreciating the fact that he was taking her fears seriously. She got out of the bed and sat on the floor in front of him so they were eye to eye, then leaned against the bed as if it were a backrest. She pulled up one knee and looped her arms around it. It was a common pose. When they had been dating, they'd spent many hours sitting on a blanket at the beach, picnicking and talking for hours. Being near the water was one of Ben's passions, and Jordan had shared that love of the ocean with him. "So how have you been?"

He raised his eyebrow, apparently surprised at her innocuous question, but he finally shrugged. "Lonely. You left a big hole in my heart. I'm still grieving your loss."

She hadn't expected such a truthful, heartfelt answer. She didn't see condemnation in his features, but the pain was clearly written across his face. "I'm so sorry I hurt you, Ben. That was not my goal, I promise you."

He waited silently for her to continue, apparently not trusting himself to speak.

It was time. And maybe by talking through her problems, she could avoid discussing the emotions that were so painful to wade through. She took a deep breath. "So, you know I was working at Southeastern Labs for the last few years in their research-and-development department. We had several trials going on with various drugs. I was working on a new medicine for migraines called Mintax. It's a neurological drug, and we were studying the effects it had on the brain. Migraines are still largely a mystery, even though millions of people suffer with them—they're even chronic in a large population. If we could discover a cure, we could make Southeastern millions and help people all over the world. Of course, the team was sworn to secrecy, and we weren't allowed to discuss the drug with anyone outside of Southeastern. Big Pharma is highly competitive, and spies have been known to poach formulas. The more we worked, the tighter the security became."

Ben nodded. "Yeah, I remember that you mentioned Mintax, but you couldn't tell me any details about the drug. I also remember that they were keeping you at the lab for long hours before you disappeared."

"Well, as we worked, we discovered that Mintax has some very unusual properties. The chemical compound is odorless, tasteless and virtually impossible to detect in the human body after it is consumed. It's even harder to find than those steroids the athletes keep trying to use to enhance their performance. After several hours, it doesn't show up in regular toxicology screens, even when taken in higher doses." She leaned forward. "But there is more. We discovered that Mintax doesn't do much for migraines after all, except for in a very small percentage of users. On top of that, in certain populations, it causes seizures and even death."

Ben raised an eyebrow. "It kills people? Are you kidding?"

"No, it's definitely not a joke. If given in the right dose, a person with various preexisting medical issues can go into seizures within about thirty minutes or so of taking the medication, depending upon certain variables, like body weight, metabolic levels, preexisting medical conditions—you know, the normal contingencies. Of those, about thirty-two percent of them die. Southeastern called that number significant. I call it appalling. Then, once the seizures stop, it's virtually impossible to prove that Mintax was the cause."

"So didn't Southeastern need to stop the drug testing and go back to the drawing board before more people got hurt?"

Jordan nodded. "That's what should have happened, but it didn't. Hence my problem. Southeastern spent a fortune developing Mintax, and they couldn't afford to go back to the drawing board. It obviously won't cure migraines for the masses as they'd hoped, so there was no future revenue available to help the company recoup their costs, and they didn't have any other big drug trials warming up in the bull pen. You have to understand, they put everything they had into the Mintax program—literally all of their eggs were in one basket. They are testing some other drugs, but nothing on the scale of Mintax. In fact, the migraine medication should never have made it to human trials in the first place, but once it did, they couldn't afford to stop. On top of everything else, I think Southeastern might be having financial problems. Do you remember Sam Delvers, the CEO of the company?"

Ben nodded. "By reputation only. I've never met the man."

"Well, at first, he would come down to the research-and-development section once every quarter or so, and my boss would take him around on a tour of the floor and give him updates on all of our research. Mr. Delvers has always been a hands-on kind of boss, wanting to see everything for himself rather than just relying on reports and projections. Once the Mintax trials began, he started showing up weekly—and then daily once we moved from testing on animals to testing on humans. But we weren't testing on normal segments of the population. My boss discovered Southeastern was using the homeless and single people without families that wouldn't be missed. They were doing extensive background checks on the people who were testing the drug, so if a death did occur, it could easily be covered up. It also meant they could fudge the numbers, and no one would be the wiser."

Ben shifted. "How did Southeastern get permission from the FDA to go to human trials so quickly? I thought new drugs had a more rigorous testing phase."

Jordan nodded, pleased that Ben had homed in so quickly on one of the biggest problems in this case. "It's supposed to. Usually it takes about twelve years and $350 million dollars to get a new drug from the lab to the shelf at your local drugstore. After a new drug is developed, it is tested in the lab for about three and a half years or so before the Food and Drug Administration will let it be tested on humans. If the FDA says it's okay, then the new drug will enter three different phases of clinical trials. During phase one, they use less than a hundred healthy people to test the drug's safety. That usually takes a year. Then, during phase two, the sample size goes up to three hundred people, and that group tests the drug's effectiveness. That takes another two years. During phase three, the sample group can go up to around three thousand, and people in clinics and hospitals try out the drug. They're supposed to be monitored very carefully to see if the drug is effective and whether or not there are any adverse reactions in the patients. This takes another three years. Then Southeastern would have to submit a new application to the FDA for final approval, which takes another two and half years or so." She paused and took a breath. "In the case of Mintax, Southeastern obviously leapfrogged some of those steps. After my boss, Jeremy Sparks, discovered that Southeastern was testing on the homeless to avoid liability and lie about the numbers, we both started digging into the paperwork. We found that the FDA approval documents were forged, as well as the effectiveness studies and claims."

Ben raised an eyebrow. "And you're sure Delvers knew that the correct procedure wasn't being followed?"

Jordan shrugged. "I'm not sure, but somebody at the top was pulling those strings. During those last few weeks, Delvers was always around, asking questions. I'm also pretty sure Sparks confronted him. I walked by my boss's office one evening, and the two were yelling at each other. I heard them mention Mintax. Sparks was also an honest, honorable man. There is no way he would have sanctioned the lies. I'm sure he would have brought them to the attention of the CEO or the board. He wouldn't have just let it slide. That's one thing I'm sure of. In fact, Sparks told me he was about to go to the FDA with the forgeries, and with the accurate results from the human trials. He was just trying to track down one or two more documents that supported his case. Then suddenly Sparks disappeared. The next thing I knew, I was reading his obituary in the paper." She shifted, her arms tightening around her leg. "It turns out Jeremy Sparks died from unexplained seizures, even though he was only in his fifties and didn't have a history of epilepsy or any other disease that would have caused them." She paused, the horror of the situation once again settling over her. Finally, she took a deep breath and pushed on. "As far as R & D goes, there were only three of us that were overseeing the Mintax program that could really tie it altogether—Jeremy, myself and Samantha Peretti, who was in charge of the human trials. Everyone else only worked on pieces of the project and really never knew the full extent of what Mintax could or couldn't do—or the scandal surrounding the trials. After Jeremy was killed, I got scared. I emptied my bank account and thought about running, but I still couldn't believe that Southeastern would hurt Sparks. I mean, he was a loyal employee, after all. And you don't usually hear about companies killing off their employees."

She bit her bottom lip, then continued, "A couple of days later, I decided I needed to talk privately with Samantha and get her take on what had happened to Sparks. She was scared and wasn't willing to see me at first. Finally, she agreed, and we set an appointment for Thursday morning. Then she died in a car accident that very day on her way into the office. When I heard, at first, I was too terrified to do anything, but then I discovered that Southeastern was cleaning house, and the entire Mintax program was shut down. All of the specimens and reports had suddenly disappeared, as well. It was as if the entire project never even existed. I knew I had to do something. I couldn't let Southeastern get away with killing Sparks and Samantha, and all of those people that participated in the human trials. I also knew that I had to disappear, too, or I would be the next one in a grave. As soon as I heard about Samantha, I went straight to the US Attorney's Office, and I'm sure someone followed me. I am convinced I wouldn't have survived the day if I hadn't left at that very moment."

"So what happened?" Ben asked.

"Apparently, Southeastern Labs was already on the US attorney's radar, and the government had been slowly building a case against the company for fraud, kidnapping and murder due to the illegal testing. Sparks had been working with the prosecution team to help with the case, so when he died, they immediately started looked for another source. After Samantha died, I became that source. They had already planned to talk to me when I walked through their door."

"What about Southeastern and the financial fallout?" Ben asked. "As you said, they spent a fortune developing Mintax. Even if they shut the program down, the company couldn't just write the losses off if they didn't have a drug to show for it—even a failed one."

Jordan's lips thinned. "I agree, but I don't know all of the ins and outs of the financial side of things. I'm not sure how Sam Delvers decided to deal with the losses. I heard something about them trying to produce it in a third world country, but I don't know if that is true or not. I really don't know what their final decision was, or how they were planning to survive the financial disaster the drug caused."

Ben was silent for a long time, and Jordan could tell that he was processing everything that she had told him. It was quite a story, and she realized it sounded far-fetched. Reputable pharmaceutical companies didn't usually resort to murder to clean up their messes, but there had been a lot going on at Southeastern—a lot she couldn't explain and was still trying to figure out. She had been high enough in the management hierarchy to know the specifics about Mintax, but not high enough to know how Southeastern had chosen to deal with the various problems the company faced as a result of the drug's failure.

Ben's eyes were intense. "So, what happened next? Did you testify against Southeastern? How did it all turn out? I haven't heard a thing about this on the news."

"Southeastern had some incredibly talented attorneys that were also unscrupulous. When they deposed me, I felt like I was the criminal. They twisted everything I said. When I finally did testify, I could tell the case wasn't going well. I don't know everything that happened because they wouldn't let me sit in the courtroom during the testimony, but I do know that the case ended up being dropped and the whole situation was basically swept under the rug. The marshals moved me to a midsize town in South Carolina, and then basically ignored me, even when I told them I saw a suspicious man following me on several occasions." She took a deep breath. "The man I was worried about kept popping up at strange places, and there was no doubt he was going to hurt me. At one point, he even tried to run me off the road." She shifted uncomfortably. "I knew it was just a matter of time before I ended up like Samantha and Jeremy. I still had some money left, so I came back to Jacksonville. Then yesterday, I saw the same man who tried to kill me in South Carolina. He followed me here."

Finally, Ben spoke, and she saw raw pain in his eyes. "I still don't understand why you didn't come to me when you heard about Sparks's and Samantha's deaths—or even before that when you first discovered there was a problem at Southeastern. You must have considered your options and decided what to do before you knocked on the door at the US Attorney's Office. I work at the Sheriff's Office. I was your fiancé. I could have protected you. We could have worked through this together. Instead, you disappeared, and I thought you were dead."

Jordan tensed and pushed some of her hair behind her ear as fear squeezed her stomach. Had her past actions destroyed Ben's willingness to help her? She knew her story sounded far-fetched, and she was asking him to take a lot on faith. As she watched his face, however, she realized that he did believe her. The problem was that her disappearance had broken his heart. How could she make him understand? She leaned forward and gently touched his arm. "You're right. I should have. I'm so sorry, and I know words aren't going to erase how much I hurt you." She removed her hand and leaned back. "I also know you're good at your job, and you could have protected me, but I was terrified. I thought that if I involved you, you would become collateral damage when they came after me, or they would come after you, too, once they realized you were a threat." She bit her bottom lip, then pushed forward. "Two of my colleagues had just been murdered. I wanted to protect you. I didn't want you killed because of me."

He took a moment to digest her words, and she could tell that he was still struggling with her explanation. He rubbed his hand across his eyes in a tired, drained motion. Finally, he spoke again. "So what changed? Why are you here now?" She could hear the hurt in his voice, and it fueled the regret she had already been feeling.

"I need help," she said softly. "I thought I could do this on my own, but I can't. The marshals wouldn't help me. And I finally realized you're the only one that can. Southeastern hurt a lot of people and developed a very nasty drug. They were never held accountable, and I'm the only one who knows it. Now Southeastern wants me dead. I didn't know what else to do or where else to go."

Ben was silent again, apparently mulling over her words. Finally, he made a decision. "Tell me what you need."

She let out a sigh of relief. She had been holding her breath, waiting for his answer, and hadn't even realized it. "I have to get proof of the Mintax drug and what it can do, and I need to bring that and what they did during the human trials out into the open so we can prove they lied about the drug's properties. I also need to show that they killed my boss and Samantha. They won't need to kill me if Mintax and Southeastern's actions are no longer a secret. But right now, it's just my word against theirs."

"And where do you propose we get this proof?"

"That I don't know. Maybe you can help me track down some people who know more than they think they do. There also has to be something left on Southeastern's computers, but they revoked my access to their servers." She shifted. "The company doesn't like loose ends. Someone there sent that man to kill me yesterday. I'm sure of it. I've been renting out a small cottage, but I've been afraid to even go out much because I knew they were searching for me." She tightened her arms around her leg once again. "When I went to the grocery store yesterday, that was the first time I'd left my place in days. When I got to the store, I saw a man following me. I don't know if he figured out where I was living or not, but I just couldn't go back and take that chance."

Ben raised an eyebrow. “Are you sure it was the same man you saw in South Carolina?”

She nodded. “Positive. When I saw him, I ran out of the grocery store, but he followed me and tried to kill me in the parking lot. I managed to escape, but he shot me in my arm, which slowed me down. I ran across the road, and he got hit by a car when he tried to follow me. I think he’s probably dead, but I don’t think it will take them long before they send someone else.”

Suddenly, they both heard the sound of glass breaking. Ben immediately grabbed his pistol and put his finger to his lips, urging her to stay silent. She nodded, her heart beating so loudly she was sure the intruder could hear it.

“Someone’s in the house,” Ben whispered. “Stay here and crawl between the bed and the wall. I’ll be back.”

FIVE

Ben low crawled toward the kitchen, his Glock in his hand. He hadn't heard any voices, but he could tell from the sound of the glass that someone had broken a windowpane in his back door, and the prowler had probably reached in and unlocked and opened the door. Still close to the floor, he glanced quickly around the hallway wall that led to his kitchen. The hall light offered some illumination, but all he could really see was the shadow of a man who was slowly entering his house with his gun drawn. The intruder seemed to be alone, and Ben hoped there was only one man to contend with instead of several. He said a silent prayer for strength and wisdom, secured his pistol in his belt, then took a breath and quickly jumped up and charged the man, reaching for his gun hand and hoping to disarm him.

The element of surprise worked in his favor, and he managed to knock the gun from the man's hand and it went flying, clattering against the floor several feet away. The trespasser didn't give up easily, though, and he landed a punch in Ben's stomach before Ben could block him. Pain radiated throughout his gut. He grimaced and prevented the next punch, then landed one of his own on the man's chin. The intruder staggered back, but shook off the blow, straightened and came at Ben again. Ben reacted quickly, his law enforcement training immediately sending him into action. Ben was a big man, but this criminal was large, as well—and obviously a well-trained adversary. He took several steps and then launched himself at Ben, tackling him around the shoulders and pushing him back against the kitchen table with the force of his attack. Ben couldn't stop his momentum, and he heard the table splintering beneath their combined weight as they fell to the floor with the broken wood. The stranger was reaching for his throat in an effort to strangle him, and Ben pushed against his hands.

Not today, Ben thought silently, and he broke the man's grip and heaved the man to the right. The intruder rolled but grabbed a broken table leg as he did so. Before Ben could stop him, he was on his feet again and threatening Ben with the table leg as if it were a baseball bat.

Ben was done playing games. He pulled out his pistol and pointed it directly at the man's midriff, even though he was still laying amongst the pieces of the broken table. "Freeze, buddy, or your next move will be your last."

The stranger stopped, motionless, and Ben tried to take in his features. He was wearing black cargo pants, army boots and a black long-sleeved T-shirt that was just tight enough to show that the man was heavily built and muscular. His eyes were dark, and he had short brown hair cut in a military style. His face was unshaven, and there was a small scar, about half an inch long, under his left eye, that had healed long ago. Ben didn't recognize the man, but he knew a formidable foe when he saw one. This aggressor wasn't someone who just happened to be burglarizing his house. If Ben had to guess, he figured the man was a hired gun sent to silence Jordan. Nothing else made sense.

As if on cue, Jordan chose that moment to come into the kitchen. "Are you okay?" she asked. "I heard…" Her voice dropped away as she saw the scene in front of her.

The criminal threw the table leg at Jordan, and it caused the distraction he needed to turn and disappear out the back door he had entered only moments before. Jordan ducked behind the wall, but not before the end of the wood caught her in her injured arm above the elbow. She cried out, and Ben instantly decided to let the man escape. Instead of chasing after him, he quickly secured his weapon in his waistband and stood, then went to Jordan's side and pulled her into an embrace. For the first time since her return, she welcomed his touch, and Ben reveled in the feel of having her in his arms once again.

"Are you okay?" He ran his fingers lightly over her arm, testing for injury. "I thought I told you to stay in the bedroom."

Jordan rubbed her wounded arm but nodded at him. "It hurts more than before, but it isn't broken. I'll be alright." She looked up into his eyes. "I heard the noise and got worried. Then when it stopped, I thought it was safe to come out. I'm so sorry—I didn't mean to cause this kind of problem for you. He must have followed me here."

"It's not your fault, Jordan. Anybody who knew even a little bit about you would have figured that you would eventually come knocking on my door. They probably had my house under surveillance, just waiting for you to appear." He shifted, still holding her close. "Now it's time to take this to law enforcement for help. I'll call Frankie, and we'll..."

"No!" she said quickly. "We can't go to the police."

Ben shook his head. "Jordan, I'm a deputy at the Sheriff's Office. That hasn't changed since you disappeared. You know that. A crime has been committed. Actually several, including the one that just happened here tonight in my own house. That means we report it. I can't just let it go."

Her eyes widened, fear mirrored back at him. She pulled away from him and wrapped her arms around her chest. "I can't go to the authorities yet," she said adamantly. "I don't have any new proof. The US attorney won't even pursue this if I can't give him something more than we had before."

"Then we find proof—the legal way. We get warrants, subpoenas, whatever we need..."

"No!" she said again, this time her voice rising in pitch. She was close to hysterics and she wrapped her arms around herself. "I can't. They'll come after all of you. This is big. Really big. Someone else will get hurt."

He took a step toward her, then another, but she backed away, still unwilling to let him in. He dropped his hands, frustrated. He was a law enforcement officer.

He couldn't just ignore what she'd told him. Her story had to be investigated. If someone at Southeastern had ordered the deaths of two scientists, they had to be held responsible. And if they had indeed created a drug that was harmful to the public and had done illegal human trials, the proper authorities needed to know about that, too, and they had to be stopped. If the Feds didn't want the case, maybe the state attorney would be willing to take a crack at it. Deciding how to move forward legally went way above his pay grade, but he knew he had a duty to delve into the case, either way. He couldn't just go on without doing his job. "I don't understand what you want from me, Jordan. I know you're scared, but you came to me for help, and I'm offering it now. Let me help you."

She leaned against the wall, clearly shaking. Without realizing it, she had backed herself into the corner. "I don't know what I expected, Ben. Maybe I was hoping you'd help investigate Southeastern off the books. It's a catch-22 situation. I need your help, but if you do, I'm putting you in danger. I'm just so tired. I can't think straight. I don't know the right answer here."

Ben's chest felt like someone was squeezing it. It hurt to see her suffering like this. She was usually so confident and sure of her choices. She still had dark circles under her eyes, even though she'd slept for a couple of hours, and she looked as if exhaustion was consuming her from the inside out. She was obviously running on fumes and stressed to the maximum. He said a silent prayer.

Dear, God, please convince her that I'm here to help. Let her trust me.

He waited another minute, and the silence stretched between them. Finally, he ran his hand through his hair and spoke again. "I've got to call Frank and report the intruder. If Southeastern is behind all of this, they won't stop now. They'll assume that we've talked and that I know what you know." He gentled his voice. "We'll take this one step at a time, okay? First, we deal with what just happened here tonight. Then we'll figure out our next move."

"*Our* next move?" she finally said softly, a question in her voice.

"Yes, *our* next move," he answered. "I'm not going to let you face this threat alone, Jordan. Somehow, we'll get to the bottom of this, and someone is going to be held accountable for those deaths. That much I promise you."

Jordan had no more patience, endurance or energy left. She moved a chair into a corner of the living room, and watched warily as the Sheriff's Office personnel stepped around the broken table and swarmed around Ben's home. Two officers were talking to Ben as they collected evidence from the gun the intruder had left behind, while a woman was dusting the door frame for fingerprints. Jordan recognized them all by sight as colleagues of Ben's that she had met while they were dating, but the only one she truly knew was Franklin Kennedy, Ben's partner. They had double-dated several times with Frank and Bailey, Frank's wife, and she had liked both of them immensely. Still, she couldn't get past the fear that something horrible would happen to them all now that they knew about Mintax and Southeastern. Her colleagues' deaths terrified her, pure and simple. In fact, before Samantha and Jeremy had died, she had never even known someone who had been murdered. The deaths had been sudden and tragic. Now she was responsible for putting even more lives at risk. But what else could she have done? She really was out of options. She had limited resources left—very little money and no house or apartment to go to where she even felt safe. Southeastern's henchmen were closing in, and the intruder tonight would have killed her for sure if Ben hadn't stopped him.

She looked at her hands and tried to keep them from trembling. What she needed was several days of rest without the stress and fear eating away at her insides. Then maybe she could think straight. She glanced up at Ben, who was still talking to Frank in low tones a few steps away. Had she done the right thing? She knew she had hurt him, but she also knew that he was her best hope of surviving this ordeal. Despite her misgivings, she was finally starting to feel a bit of confidence in her choice to confide in him.

Could he forgive her? Someday he might, but she had shattered his trust. She could see it in his eyes every time he looked at her. He would certainly never want to have a relationship with her again, and if or when this case was closed, she would have to start over somewhere new. There were too many memories in Jacksonville that would assault her every time she thought about Ben and everything she had thrown away. Just driving over the bridges would remind her of all of the walks they had taken by the river, watching the dolphins and just enjoying each other's company. Seeing the ocean would remind her of the weekends they had spent taking his boat out, fishing in the Atlantic or just jumping the waves as they water-skied.

She shifted uncomfortably.

She might have lost her relationship with a wonderful man, but at least she was still alive. She couldn't forget that. Her colleagues had paid the ultimate price for their involvement with Mintax. She had to honor their memory by pushing forward and proving Southeastern's culpability. But could she find the proof she needed to substantiate her claims? The doubt ate her up inside. She was used to doing everything herself and never asking for help, but this time, she recognized that she was in over her head. But perhaps with Ben's help, it would be possible to stop Southeastern before anyone else got hurt. Then, maybe, she could resume her life somewhere else.

"Jordan?"

Ben's voice pulled her out of her thoughts, and she glanced up and met his eyes. "Yes?"

"It's late, and we're just about done here. I'm going to take you to a hotel I know where you will be safe, okay? Then tomorrow, we'll take your statement and start digging into this case."

"Okay, Ben." She watched him as he turned and spoke again to Frank and another detective from their team. She had always thought Ben was the most handsome man alive, and that opinion hadn't changed now that she saw him in action, taking control of this situation with ease. A whisper of attraction swept through her. His dark brown hair was styled in a military cut, and his chocolate-brown eyes were filled with acumen and intelligence. His forehead was broad, his cheekbones high and his features were finely chiseled and very masculine. His size probably intimidated some, but she loved the fact that his shoulders were wide, his legs were long and he was well over six feet tall. Many probably wouldn't describe him as handsome. His attributes were a bit too strong. But he made her heart flutter with the simplest of looks or touches. He was also a gentle giant, and as sweet as could be on the inside.

Their relationship was over, though. She tamped down the feelings of loss that had suddenly tightened in her chest. She had to keep her focus. Discovering the truth about Mintax—that was the goal. Their quest for the truth was the only thing that mattered.

After a few more verbal exchanges, Ben was ready to go. He led her out the door and to his unmarked sedan, which was parked in front of his house. He helped her get settled in the front seat, then circled the car, threw a duffel bag with a change of clothes and some toiletries in the backseat, and got in the driver's seat. "Ready?"

"As ready as I can be."

He started the engine and headed toward the hotel, and she looked cautiously around as they drove. She didn't see any threats or anyone following them, but somewhere out there, she knew the man who had broken into Ben's house was watching them—and probably reporting everything that was happening to someone at Southeastern who was plotting her death at this very moment.

SIX

Donald Eddy, or just plain "Eddy" to most of his colleagues, leaned back in his chair. He was one of the assistant state attorneys for the Fourth Judicial Circuit in Jacksonville and regularly worked with Ben and Frank on cases. He had been one of Ben's first calls that morning, right after he had talked to the US attorney in downtown Jacksonville, and the marshal's office. The Feds had been very closemouthed about the entire case, but they had promised to send down someone to talk to him and the sheriff at some point. In the meantime, Ben wanted Eddy looped in from the beginning as they started their investigation, regardless of how the Feds wanted to proceed. Eddy's legal mind sometimes caught things that Ben's law enforcement background didn't focus on, and Ben knew that Eddy was a valuable part of their team.

"Well I found out that Southeastern was slapped with a series of fines for failing to comply with the federal drug approval process. Apparently, they worked out a plea agreement, and that was basically the end result of the legal action against them. They tried to hold Sam Delvers, the CEO, responsible as well, but nothing stuck. And jeopardy attached—neither one can be charged again with anything related to the FDA case."

Jordan put her hands up in the air. "What? Fines are the going punishment these days for killing people?"

Eddy shuffled some papers on his desk. "The case had nothing to do with any murders. Apparently, Southeastern claimed they had applied for expedited approval, but the paperwork was somehow misplaced by the FDA. They also claimed none of the documents were forged, but that, somehow, drafts had been mistakenly submitted that hadn't been finalized. They also acknowledged that Mintax had failed one clinical trial, but that it had passed the second after the standards were revised, even though it showed minimal benefit. Believe it or not, Mintax was well on its way to being approved before the US attorney stepped in. They weren't able to get criminal sanctions, but they did manage to keep Mintax off the store shelves, at least for now."

Ben put his hand on Jordan's knee, hoping to calm her. She looked like a firecracker whose fuse had just been lit. "Well, the forgery was just the tip of the iceberg, anyway," she said, her voice acerbic. "What about the murders? What about using the homeless for the clinical trials?"

Eddy cleared his throat. "Well, those cases were apparently dismissed before jeopardy attached, so if you find evidence that points to someone specific, we can still try to go after the guilty parties. The judge said no to my search warrant for Southeastern's records, though. She said there's not enough probable cause. Yet."

"What?" Jordan brushed Ben's hand away, jumped to her feet and started pacing back and forth across the back of the attorney's office, her face changing from white to red in only a few seconds. "That has to be a mistake."

Ben wasn't too surprised, but he motioned for Jordan to come back to her chair. "Let's hear the man out."

Jordan clenched her fists as she walked, but she finally returned to the chair she had vacated shortly before. "Isn't it obvious? Southeastern is out of control. Someone from the lab was even behind the attack at Ben's house!"

Eddy steepled his fingers. "There's nothing to prove that, and nothing to connect the two legally. To be honest, I don't have enough at this point to go after Southeastern on any front, Ms. Kendrick. I need more than your sworn affidavit that Mintax causes seizures like you described and that the lab is responsible for the death of your two colleagues. Reports, witnesses, corroborating testimony—anything that substantiates your claim. The Feds are acting like they're done with this case and aren't going to pursue it any further, and they're notorious for not wanting to share their files, so we're basically starting from scratch. So far, everything you've told me is circumstantial. As far as what happened at Deputy Graham's house, I have proof that someone broke in and attacked him, but I don't have anything that ties that event to Southeastern except your belief that it's true. I can't even prove that you were the target. As far as the law is concerned, it could have been a random break-in."

"Random my foot!" She motioned to her arm. "Well, what about the guy who shot me in front of the grocery store? He was from Southeastern, too. Did anyone do a background check or try to find out who hired him? It had to be Sam Delvers or someone else at Southeastern. That link should be easy to prove."

"Since he died from his injuries before anyone could take his statement, we haven't learned much," Ben said softly. "There was no match on his prints. So far, we haven't been able to prove anything apart from the fact that he was definitely chasing you. Several witnesses confirmed your story. That investigation is still ongoing, but we haven't uncovered anything that ties him to Delvers or Southeastern. We haven't even been able to identify him yet."

Eddy leaned forward. "The judge wants proof, and she won't budge until she gets it."

"Well how are we supposed to get that proof if we can't search Southeastern's records?" Jordan asked, her voice still bitter.

"We'll find a way," Ben said softly. "Remember, we just started our investigation." He reached out and touched Jordan's arm, hoping to calm her. He'd guessed that it was too early in the investigation to approach the judge, but Jordan had insisted on asking for the search warrants right away, and it didn't hurt to have Eddy on board from the beginning. Ben knew that Eddy was dedicated and tenacious, and once they built a case against Southeastern, Eddy would do everything in his power to not only win but obtain justice. But Ben also knew they had a lot of work in front of them.

He glanced over at Eddy, who was reviewing the file on his desk. Eddy was good at explaining things to people, and Ben hoped that he could give Jordan some peace of mind. Eddy's next words confirmed that he had made the right decision by coming here today.

"Look, Ms. Kendrick," the attorney said in a professional tone. "For the record, I believe everything you've told me today. You've scared me—and I don't scare easily. This case is huge, and Southeastern has to be stopped. They also have to pay for the deaths of Jeremy Sparks and Samantha Peretti, if they were indeed responsible. The Feds seemed to have focused on the drug trials and FDA forgeries for their case, but I want to focus on the deaths that happened right here in Florida. I don't need the Feds to go forward. But what I do need is proof. Your statement is a great beginning, but I need more to satisfy the judge so we can get access to Southeastern's records. If you can get me some witnesses that can confirm what you're saying and make the connections, or proof that Southeastern or someone within the company hired the man who tried to kill you, then I will take that to the judge and try to get the warrant again. Show me something that ties the man who broke into Ben's house to Southeastern. A payment for services will do, or proof of a conversation with someone who ordered the man to go after you and Ben. Okay?"

Ben stood and shook Eddy's hand, then put his hand

behind Jordan's back. "Thanks for trying, Eddy. We'll be in touch."

As soon as they cleared the attorney's office, Jordan turned, her face revealing her frustration. "Well, you were right. We need a lot more."

"Don't give up. We'll get more."

"Well, where do we start?"

Ben smiled. "We start with my team. Like I said before, I work with a good group of deputies. They're the best in Florida. If anyone can get to the bottom of this, it's them." He took a step to the left so he could catch her eye. Her frustration and anger were clearly written all over her face. He hoped she wouldn't try to go it alone or disappear on him again, just because they'd hit their first bump in the road. "What are you thinking?" he asked cautiously.

Jordan shrugged, obviously dejected. "I'm thinking the same thing I thought before. It's dangerous to have so many people working on this case. Southeastern will come after anyone and everyone that they see as a threat. Every deputy in your office will be in danger the minute they start the investigation, and now even Eddy is at risk, too."

"Well, that's what we do, Jordan. Our job entails danger every single day. Working the Southeastern case is par for the course."

Jordan shook her head. "It's not the same, and I don't want you to minimize the threat. Southeastern is a multimillion-dollar corporation that wields a large amount of power. They won't go down without a fight, and it's obvious that they're not afraid to break the law.

In my book, that makes them even more dangerous than your average criminal. Look at that guy who broke into your house. He was no lightweight Delvers hired on a whim. He was a professional. I don't know much about mercenaries, but he sure seemed to fit the bill."

Ben nodded. "We knew what we were signing up for when we took this job, Jordan. If it were easy, everyone would do it. Let's go talk to Frankie and get him up to speed."

Jordan felt like there was a balloon in her chest—one that kept expanding until it was sure to pop and explode. She glanced over at Ben as he drove them back to the Sheriff's Office. His features were schooled into a professional mask, and his lips were drawn into a thin line of determination. He certainly had stepped up to the plate and was now neck-deep in the investigation, just as he'd promised. Despite the stress she felt, she was also incredibly glad that she no longer had to deal with this Southeastern mess on her own. It had been simply too much for her to bear, and it was a giant relief to have help and a team of professionals on her side. For the first time in months, she had confidence that Southeastern would actually be held accountable for their crimes and stopped from hurting anybody else.

Even though she was comforted, the fact that she had to depend upon others still ate away at her. She had always been fiercely independent and wanted to do everything herself. She was smart, strong and capable. Yet, this entire experience was slowly teaching her humility. On some level, she knew that she couldn't stop Southeastern on her own, and at times, that concept was a bitter pill to swallow. She said a silent prayer, thanking God for protecting her and for bringing Ben into her life to help her with this fight.

She glanced over at Ben again and another whisper of attraction swept over her, as well as a sensation of regret. It had felt so good when he had held her in his arms after the break-in, yet the more time they spent together, the more obvious it became that their relationship was irretrievably broken. She hadn't had the nerve to ask him if he'd moved on and found a new relationship. Deep down, she was afraid of the answer. If he said yes, she didn't think she could take it. But even without a new girlfriend, she saw the pain in Ben's eyes every time he looked at her. She briefly closed her own eyes and tried to force her thoughts back to the case.

They arrived back at the Sheriff's Department and met up with Frank and the rest of Ben's team. After the attack last night, Ben had gotten permission from the chief at the Sheriff's Office to investigate the Southeastern case and to keep Jordan in protective custody, which allowed Ben and his team to work with Jordan with the department's blessing. Today, they started to methodically map out a plan of action. Two other detectives would go over every detail, no matter how small, of the drug trial. They were going to investigate the use of the homeless, how the people were recruited and the results in comparison to what was actually reported. Their first step was to identify and interview any of the victims and their families.

Jordan glanced over at Bailey, Frank's wife, who

worked on the internet-and-technology team at the Sheriff's Office. Frank and Bailey were tasked with trying to track down the intruder that had broken into Ben's house, and finding a connection, if any, between him, the man who shot Jordan and someone that worked at Southeastern. Both investigations were going to be an uphill climb since there was little to no physical evidence available, but Jordan was delighted that Bailey would be helping them.

She watched surreptitiously and saw Bailey wink at Frank, who gave her a soft smile in return. Although they had been married for over a year, Jordan could still see the sparks of attraction flying between the two whenever they were together. Bailey had encountered Frank when her father, a private investigator, was killed about two years ago. He had been researching the backgrounds of the five applicants vying for the CEO position for a different pharmaceutical company that also operated in the Jacksonville area, Gates Pharmaceuticals. Gates sometimes distributed drugs developed at Southeastern's labs, but besides that small connection, Gates and Southeastern were separate companies with totally different corporate infrastructures and leadership. Gates had been the target of a man who wanted to use the corporation as a front for an illegal enterprise and to launder money. He was now dead, and after a full investigation by the FBI and Interpol, Gates was under the leadership of a new CEO that was taking the company in a new and better direction.

After a rough start, Bailey had eventually been allowed to assist with the investigation of her father's murder. As she and Frank had worked together, their relationship grew and they fell in love, despite Frank's background in law enforcement and Bailey's history of breaking the law. Bailey had changed her ways and had really become an asset to the Sheriff's Office. She was an extremely talented computer hacker, and her skills at the keyboard had already been key in solving several cases since she had joined their team. According to Ben, she had no equal in the entire division. Jordan was confident that if anyone could dig out the proof that might be available electronically, it would be Bailey with Frank's sharp mind helping her along the way.

She glanced over at Ben, who had just finished telling everyone their assignments. They had already decided to start the official inquiry by interviewing Jeremy Sparks's widow, Emma. Jordan wasn't convinced she really knew anything about what was going on at Southeastern, but they had to start somewhere. Emma hadn't been willing to talk to Jordan when she had contacted her in the past, but she had agreed to meet with Ben this afternoon since he was a law enforcement officer. Jordan hoped that Emma would not only open up about Mintax and Southeastern, if she knew anything, but that she would also allow an autopsy of her husband. Although Mintax was virtually impossible to detect after ingestion, Jordan hoped that fresh eyes and a pathology expert might find something they had missed in their own labs. It was entirely possible that today's visit might yield nothing of value, but it was worth a try.

After the meeting at the Sheriff's Office concluded and everyone had their marching orders, Jordan and

Ben headed out for the interview. The Sparkses owned a home out in the country north of Jacksonville and close to the Georgia state line, and it took over half an hour to reach the dirt road that led back to their property. Jordan checked the GPS on her phone to verify that they were actually turning off on the correct street. The area seemed deserted, and she wondered, not for the first time, if they were even in the right area. They had turned where the GPS led them, but they didn't see a single house or other car as they drove. After about ten minutes or so of traveling along the dirt road, Jordan began to get worried. "Are you sure we're in the right place? It feels like we're out in the boonies."

"No, I'm not sure," Ben answered, "but you are my navigator. What is the GPS saying now?"

"It says we should have already reached the house. Maybe we should ask for directions?"

"I'd be happy to—if we could find someone to ask. I don't see too many neighbors out here, though."

"Watch out!" A black sedan suddenly seemed to come out of nowhere, and was heading straight for them at a high rate of speed. Ben slowed and tried to pull out of the car's way, but the sedan kept coming right down the middle of the road. At the last possible second, Ben swerved even farther to the right, avoiding the collision but ending up on the overgrown shoulder with the car tilted precariously into the ditch. A plume of dust and sand filled the air as their car came to a hard stop, inches away from a stand of trees that canopied the area.

Ben quickly put one hand on his pistol grip as he kept his eyes on the car that had run them off the road.

It didn't stop and sped away behind them. Once the car was out of sight, he returned his hands to the wheel and tried to get the car back on the road. The tires spun against the dirt and struggled to regain purchase on the narrow thoroughfare, and for a moment, they were stuck in the sand. Finally, the tread caught the ground and surged the car back up onto the main part of the road. Jordan moved her eyes to the side mirror, fully expecting the black car to turn around and try again to crash into them or to threaten them in some other way. To her surprise, it didn't return. She sighed in relief.

"I didn't get the tag number," Ben said. "Did you happen to get it?"

"No," Jordan answered as she turned back to face him. "I tried, but everything happened so fast, I didn't get a great look. Could you tell who was driving?"

Ben shook his head. "The driver was by himself, and I believe he was a white male. That's about all I could see. I was focused on keeping our car from running into the trees." He glanced her way again. "Are you okay?"

Jordan nodded. "Yeah. I'm just relieved that we didn't crash and he didn't stick around to talk." She glanced once again at the road behind them. "Why do you think he was in such a hurry?"

They turned a corner, and when Jordan looked forward again, she saw a two-story farmhouse in the distance. She glanced at the GPS screen. The house had to belong to the Sparkses. There was nothing else around. But she had an ominous feeling that they weren't going to find anything good once they passed over the threshold.

SEVEN

Jordan and Ben made their way up the driveway and parked in front of the wraparound porch. Hot Florida humidity swept over them as they approached the front door and rang the buzzer. No one answered. Ben checked his watch and hit the doorbell again, then raised his eyebrow. "That's odd. I just talked to her before we left. She knew we were coming and said she'd be expecting us."

Jordan shrugged and brushed away a bug that was flying near her face. "We're a couple of minutes later than we expected. Maybe she got busy on a project or something."

Ben reached for the doorknob and instead of finding it locked, discovered that the door wasn't even latched. He barely touched it and the door swung open on its own. Jordan sucked in a breath as Ben drew his weapon and motioned for her to stay behind him. She shuddered as a sudden tingle swept down her spine. Something was wrong. Very wrong. She could feel it.

"Hello? Mrs. Sparks? Sheriff's Office. Are you home?"

They pushed through the front door, and Jordan

stayed cautiously behind Ben, her eyes wide and watchful.

"Mrs. Sparks? Sheriff's Office. Call out if you're here."

They passed the foyer and entered the living room.

Suddenly, Jordan screamed.

Mrs. Sparks lay dead on a carpet in front of the sofa, a bullet wound bleeding from her chest. Her eyes were still open, and her face showed a mixture of surprise and fear.

Ben put up his hand, and Jordan instantly put her hand over her mouth and quieted, even though adrenaline was pulsing through her. She hadn't meant to scream, and fully understood Ben's warning. There could still be perpetrators in the house, and since they'd killed once, they probably wouldn't hesitate to kill again. He moved closer to the woman's body and reached down to feel for a pulse, but Jordan knew there was little hope that the woman was still alive. Ben met her eye and shook his head, then kept his weapon out and led her out of the room and toward the kitchen. She felt numb inside. She hadn't really known the woman, yet she still felt the loss keenly.

The kitchen was empty, but smelled wonderfully of baking and vanilla, and a tray of cookies was still cooling on a rack by the oven. Ben verified that the oven was turned off, then continued his search, and Jordan followed closely behind him. The house was quiet except for the humming of the refrigerator and the air conditioner as it clicked on and pushed a gentle breeze through the vents.

They cleared the house in a few short minutes, methodically checking room by room, and finally Ben seemed satisfied that they were alone. He holstered his weapon and called in the murder. While he made his report, Jordan started looking around, hoping to find some clue about what had happened. The house had been ransacked, and the floor and furniture were cluttered with books, papers and other items that had been thrown around during the criminal's search.

Ben finished his call and joined her. "I wonder what they were looking for?" he asked.

"Jeremy probably wouldn't have had any hard copies of the reports dealing with the work at Southeastern," Jordan responded absently. "He liked to do all of his work on computers. But I wouldn't be surprised if he'd saved scans or other documents and copied them on a hard drive. Maybe that's what the killer was looking for. I doubt Jeremy would have used the cloud. He said over and over again that he didn't think that it was safe to store important documents there because he was worried about security." She glanced around the living room. "Do you see a laptop anywhere? Jeremy used to carry one back and forth from the office to home. Whoever did this might have also been looking for that, and if they found it, I'm sure they'd have taken it with them, just to make sure there was nothing incriminating on it. I tried asking Mrs. Sparks about the laptop months ago, but she would never agree to see me."

Ben's brow furrowed. "You're assuming this murder has something to do with Southeastern."

Jordan widened her eyes. "You're not?"

Ben shrugged. "The timing is suspicious, that I grant you. But let's not jump to any conclusions before we take a look at the evidence." He pulled out two sets of rubber gloves and handed one to Jordan, then gave her a thin pair of booties to slide over her shoes. "Put these on just in case, but try not to touch anything. Let's do another walk-through and see if you see any computers or hard drives, or any good hiding places that we might want to search once the rest of the team arrives."

She raised her eyebrows. "You know a hard drive is pretty small, right? Even the ones with a lot of storage space are only about the size of a deck of cards. Jeremy could have hidden one in a hundred different places."

Ben shrugged. "I'm aware. It may seem impossible, but if we find something, it could blow this case right open." He gave her an encouraging smile. "It's worth a try."

Jordan appreciated his efforts. It was horrific to see Mrs. Sparks murdered in her own home, but they had to push forward, and Jordan knew he was trying his best to keep her mind off the violence that had occurred only a short time before they arrived. She couldn't help Mrs. Sparks now, but she could and would keep trying to solve the case.

Still, seeing Mrs. Sparks's sightless eyes made her stomach churn, and she swayed a little as she saw them again and again in her mind's eye. Ben noticed and quickly reached over and steadied her with his hands on her arms, careful not to touch her healing wound. "Are you okay?" he asked, his tone worried.

She nodded. "I don't see dead bodies very often. This is all new to me."

He gave her arms a gentle squeeze. "That's understandable. I'm sorry you have to see all of this in the first place. Do you want to go sit in the car and wait for me? It's going to be a while before I can leave."

She shook her head. "No, I'll be okay." She took a deep breath. "Shall we start the search?"

He nodded and they headed for the guest bedroom and slowly made a perusal of each room in the house. Jordan lingered over the photos on the dresser in the master bedroom. There were several framed shots of Jeremy and his wife, and a few of a small girl that was a baby in some pictures and as big as three years old in others. She had curly brown hair and big brown eyes and was the spitting image of Jeremy and his wife.

Jordan frowned. She never realized that Jeremy had a child. He never talked about the girl, or even mentioned anyone in his family besides his wife. Maybe the child was a niece or cousin? She kept walking, stepping over items that were strewn around on the carpet. Someone had taken a knife to the overstuffed chair that had been in the corner, and stuffing and pieces of upholstery were strewn around. She now understood the analogy of a needle in a haystack. How could they figure out where Jeremy could have hidden such a small item in such a big house? The possibilities were endless. And who knew if the murderers had already found it when they did their search after killing Mrs. Sparks?

She left Ben walking toward the kitchen and went into the master bath. They had an oversized shower with beautiful marbled tiles and large glass windows. Both the door to the cabinet under the sink and the medicine cabinet were already open, and it was obvious that someone had ransacked both areas. She took a peek as well but didn't see anything out of the ordinary. The air conditioner clicked on again, and she paused a moment, letting the refreshing breeze hit her face. She turned and started to leave when she glanced up and noticed the air vent on the ceiling. There was dust gathered in the panes, but there was one section of the vent that had very little dust, and it was a rectangular shape about five by three inches wide.

"Ben?" She moved to the doorway and called across the house, and a few moments later, Ben appeared.

"I just heard from Frank. They're on their way and should be here in about half an hour or less. Did you find something?"

She pointed to the ceiling. "It might be nothing, but it looks like something is blocking the air in that vent."

Ben studied it from a couple of different angles. "It definitely looks like something might be up there. Once the rest of the team gets here, we'll check it out. The size fits." He smiled. "Good eye!" He reached out and patted her back affectionately, then pulled back quickly as if he'd been burned. The air felt thick, and Jordan was suddenly very interested in the dirt on her shoe.

"Let's keep looking, just in case I'm wrong," she said awkwardly. She slid past him and he slowly followed her, allowing the space to grow between them as they continued to move through other parts of the house. The uneasiness between them eventually dissipated, but it took longer than she'd thought, and once again, she pushed her thoughts back to the case. It was just too painful to keep thinking about her lost relationship with Ben.

She finished checking a cabinet by the TV and stopped for a moment, remembering Jeremy and the many times she had enjoyed working with him on the various projects at Southeastern. He had always been very professional, and quick to explore an idea or try something new.

She glanced around the room and sighed. It felt strange to be in Jeremy's home and going through his personal things. And now his wife was dead, too. A wave of sadness swept over her. So much death and destruction—and for what?

She checked the last cabinet and then shut it with a snap. She and Ben had searched everywhere they could think of, but neither of them had found a laptop or tablet anywhere in the house. If Jeremy's laptop had been there before they arrived, she was certain that the perpetrators must have taken it.

A few minutes later, the rest of the team arrived. Ben and Frank went back to the bathroom with a screwdriver and evidence bags, just in case, and Jordan followed them and watched as they pulled off the vent cover.

"Do you see anything?" she asked, her tone hopeful.

Ben carefully removed a small rectangular box that had been resting there and handed it to Frank, who put it in a plastic bag and sealed it. It was a small hard drive, but the cord was missing. Jordan's heart leaped at the sight. Finally, they had something that might help with the investigation. It might contain nothing, or it could contain the proof they needed to stop Southeastern before they hurt someone else.

"Amazing find, Jordan," Ben praised again as he marked the date and time the hard drive was found on the outside of the plastic bag with a permanent marker. "It's no wonder the killers didn't find it. I doubt we would've even found it without your help." He gave her a smile. "You're quite a detective."

"I can't wait to get this back to Bailey and our tech team to see what's on it," Frank added. "You'd think that if Jeremy Sparks felt like it was important enough to hide, then it must contain some valuable information." He turned it over and studied it carefully. "It's pretty dusty, and it looks like it has been here for a while. Hopefully, this is a big step toward proving Jordan's story."

"I sure hope so." Jordan smiled.

Despite the smile, Ben could see the sadness in her eyes. It was hard to be happy about the find when Mrs. Sparks lay dead in the next room. He turned to Frank. "Is there any news about the car that tried to run us off the road?"

"No," Frank answered grimly. "We sent out an all-points bulletin and have been searching, but we haven't found it yet, and since neither of you got the tag, realistically, we have little hope of finding it. One thing we do know for sure. You and Jordan are making someone nervous. I'm just sorry that you didn't get here soon enough to stop Mrs. Sparks's murder. The coroner said she's only been dead for an hour or less."

The framed photo of Jeremy and Mrs. Sparks caught Ben's eye as the group headed back toward the living room of the house. The couple in the picture were smiling as if they didn't have a care in the world, and yet now both of them were dead. He wondered if they would have lived life differently if they'd known their lives would be cut so horribly short. There was a lesson here—it was important to live each day to the fullest. He thought back to an old movie he had seen as a teenager. What had the catchphrase been—seize the day? Despite everything that had happened, he knew he did have quite a bit to be thankful for, and he needed to seize the day today and every day and appreciate those around him.

He glanced over at Jordan, who was deep in conversation with Frank. Something he said made her smile again and nod in agreement. She was so beautiful, even dressed casually in jeans and a floral top. He loved the way she was graceful with even the simplest of movements and could light up a room just by entering it. Yet, he didn't know how to breach the awkwardness that had sprang up between them, or even if it was possible to do so. He turned back to the framed pictures and studied them again before he made a fool out of himself and said something dumb in front of Frank and his colleagues.

Please help us discover the truth, Lord, Ben prayed. *Before Southeastern kills somebody else.*

EIGHT

Bailey Kennedy pushed back from the table, her face filled with frustration.

"Well?" Ben asked, his tone hopeful. "Can you see what's on the hard drive?"

"Right now, no," Bailey replied. "Eventually, I hope so."

"What's the problem?" Jordan asked, moving forward so she could get a better look at the screen. She sighed. Getting closer hadn't helped. She could tell Bailey had been working on something, but she was no computer expert, and it all looked like gibberish to her.

"The problem is, the hard drive is encrypted," Bailey said as she motioned toward the screen. "And it's no ordinary encryption program that is keeping me out. This is one called Honey Encryption. I need the key code to get in, and without it, I'm forced to guess at the code. If I guess incorrectly, the program starts sending me fake data, which makes me think I'm going in the right direction, when actually, I'm getting buried by false trails and incorrect responses. At the same time, the real code gets buried even deeper and becomes harder to discover. After hours of working on it and getting signal after signal that I was getting close, I just found out I've been going down the wrong path, and now I have to start from scratch all over again. It makes me want to beat my head against a rock!"

Ben smiled and nudged her shoulder playfully. "Don't do that! There is very little in the computer world that you can't tackle, Bailey. I have no doubt that you will conquer this latest challenge as well, even if it takes you a few days and the answers weren't readily apparent." He glanced over at Jordan. "Any guesses as to what the key code might be? You actually knew the man. You might know the answer without even realizing it."

Jordan shook her head. "I have no idea. What are normal key codes like? Are they the same as a password?" She knew how to do quite a bit on the computer, but her skills were only rudimentary compared to Bailey's.

"No," Bailey replied. "Not usually. A password can be used as a key code, but usually keys are not something that a person will remember. They're used by the software that is implementing the cryptographic algorithm, and oftentimes they are a combination of letters and numbers that seem nonsensical. There are a few crypto systems that use passwords as an encryption key, but they don't use the password to perform the primary encryption. Instead, the program uses the password as a starting point and then it will generate the actual secure encryption key itself once the password is entered. This might be one of those, but I'm not sure yet. All I can tell so far is that the access code it is requesting has twenty-five numbers or letters. They can be in any combination, and there are a huge number of possibilities. I've got a computer program working on it, but it's going to take a while." She met Jordan's eye. "You wouldn't happen to know any twenty-five-letter phrases the man was fond of saying, would you?"

Jordan shrugged. "His wife's name? His birthday? What are the most common passwords?"

"Any word, number or phrase that might be important to him. The problem is, with this program, the more I guess, the more it locks me out, so if you can point me in the right direction, it would really be helpful."

Jordan bit her bottom lip thoughtfully. "I'll try to figure it out. Jeremy wasn't the kind of guy to keep a list of passwords or key codes in his desk drawer. He liked things simple. Whatever encryption he was using, it would probably have a password-generated key that he could easily remember instead of a nonsensical code. He would have wanted it to be a piece of cake to access the device so he could focus on his work. He wouldn't have wanted to spend time trying to remember some convoluted code or be forced to look it up every time he wanted to work with a file from the hard drive. He was methodical that way, and very focused. We could search his house from top to bottom and would probably never discover the password or encryption key spelled out for us on a slip of paper," Jordan replied.

"You're probably right," Bailey said as she took a drink from a nearby cup of lemonade. "Most people just memorize their passwords and phrases. He sounds like the same type of guy."

"So," Ben said, "the bottom line is that you need more time."

Bailey smiled and put down her cup. "Exactly. It's a wonderful challenge, but I do understand that time is of the essence, so I will do my best to figure out how to access the drive as quickly as possible."

A knock on the office door caught Ben's attention, and he turned to see his chief standing at the doorway.

"Ben, I need you to come with me," he said as he motioned with his hands down the hallway. "Ms. Kendrick, you stay here."

Jordan glanced at Ben and raised her eyebrow, then motioned to the chief with her hands. "Is anything wrong?" she asked.

"No," the senior officer replied. "But there are some people in my office that Ben needs to meet."

Bailey turned back to her computer. "Ben, I'll let you know when I come up with something," she said distractedly, her mind apparently already back on the encryption puzzle and sifting through the various possibilities. "Jordan, why don't you take a seat and see if you can come up with any twenty-five-letter or twenty-five-number combinations that might have meant something to Sparks? If we work together, we just might figure this out."

"Sure thing," Jordan replied as she grabbed a nearby pad and went to work.

"Thanks for all your help, Bailey," Ben said over his

shoulder. He hesitated for a moment before following the chief down the corridor and past the conference room into the chief's office. He didn't know what to expect, but his chief wouldn't have pulled him away if it wasn't important.

There were three people waiting for them that stood when they entered. One was a woman dressed professionally in a navy suit and white blouse, who stood next to an older man wearing a black jacket with a burgundy tie who had a graying goatee. The last person was Donald Eddy, the local assistant state attorney. Eddy was standing apart from the other two, and he had a serious, almost angry expression on his face. Whatever the three had been talking about while they had waited for Ben to arrive hadn't been pleasant, if Eddy's expression was anything to go by.

The chief motioned with his hands again as he talked. "Deputy Graham, I believe you know Assistant State Attorney Donald Eddy." He pointed to the man with the burgundy tie. "And this is Sam Delvers, the CEO of Southeastern Labs." He nodded toward the woman. "This is Suzanne Tammington, one of Mr. Delvers's attorneys." He pulled the door closed behind him, then went and sat behind his desk as the group greeted each other.

Ben shook hands with each of them, then unbuttoned his jacket and took a seat as the others sat, as well. He made eye contact and nodded to Eddy, then turned toward the man with the goatee. "What can we do for you, Mr. Delvers?"

Mr. Delvers smiled but didn't say a word. Instead, Ms.

Tammington spoke up. "We understand you're investigating Southeastern, and we'd like to know why. You must realize Southeastern has already been investigated and fined for sidestepping a few minor federal regulations when the company was navigating Mintax through the drug approval process." She leaned back. "That isn't a secret, and we've learned from our mistakes. The company has paid the fine and put that nasty mess behind us. We worked with the federal agencies as much as possible and were extremely accommodating and open during their inquiries. As far as we are concerned, the matter is over, and we've moved on to greener pastures. If you have questions, we're happy to answer them so we can put your minds at ease."

"We still have some questions of state law to sort out," Eddy said, his voice professional. "It's an ongoing investigation, so I'm afraid we're not at liberty to discuss the details at this time."

Ms. Tammington crossed her legs. "The Feds thought they had more, and yet their entire case fell apart during the trial. Even the witnesses they called were weak and inefficient, and they didn't have nearly enough evidence for a conviction of any sort." She leaned forward. "I understand you've been in contact with Jordan Kendrick?"

Neither Ben nor Eddy reacted or replied, and both men kept their expressions stoic. Ms. Tammington waited a moment as she glanced at the two men, then continued, "What makes you think you can do better than someone with the full force and weight of the United States government behind them?"

Ben finally glanced back at Eddy, who just smiled.

He looked totally unruffled by the woman's words, even though Ben knew that Eddy was probably burning on the inside. The woman's comments were infuriating, but it was her body language and tone that were the most insulting. It was almost as if she were daring them to do their worst, because she was confident they would fail.

Well, they would just see about that.

Ben took in the full measure of the attorney who sat before him. Her clothes screamed tailored and expensive, and she had a gold Rolex on her wrist and a large diamond pendant around her throat. He could see her studying his jacket and tie and mentally measuring his own tastes and lack of wealth against her own. Her lip curled in disdain. She probably made his entire annual salary in less than a month, but having a large bank account didn't impress him. It was a person's heart and actions that mattered, not one's salary. "Did you have anything further, Ms. Tammington?" Ben asked, making sure his voice was calm and friendly. There was no reason to antagonize her, regardless of how she was treating them.

She raised an eyebrow. "Well, as I said, we are happy to cooperate. If we could help you close this matter once and for all, you only need to ask. Why don't you tell us specifically what you are looking for, and we'll see if we can accommodate you?"

Ben shook his head. "I'm afraid we are going in circles. As Mr. Eddy already stated, we can't comment at this time." He started to stand but stopped when Ms. Tammington spoke again.

"Detective, Southeastern is a very large company

with millions of dollars in assets. We have an army of attorneys ready and waiting to fight whatever you throw at us. You may think that you have the upper hand, but that just isn't true. The wise move here would be to close this case and try working on something else that you might actually have a chance of winning."

Eddy's smile grew wider. "A challenge. I like that." He stood. "Ms. Tammington, I can't tell you what a joy it has been to meet you and Mr. Delvers today. Thanks so much for stopping by. If you're ever in the area again, do stop in and say hello." He shrugged. "Or not. Either way, have a good day." He nodded to the chief. "Chief. I'll be in my office if you need me." He nodded to Ben and left, leaving the office door open behind him.

"I hope that attorney isn't representative of the best of your team," Ms. Tammington said under her breath as she looked at the chief. "He seems like a bit of a loose cannon."

Sam Delvers had a stony expression on his face, despite the confidence his attorney was spouting. He suddenly spoke up in a raspy, tight voice. "Fighting unnecessary legal battles is expensive and time-consuming. If you persist in prosecuting either me or Southeastern, we'll make your life miserable, and you'll only find yourself on the losing side of an embarrassing lawsuit and the six o'clock news."

The chief leaned forward and rested his elbows on his desk. "Are you threatening me, Mr. Delvers?"

"Not at all," Ms. Tammington said quickly as she put a hand on her client's arm in a show of restraint. "In fact, we are here in a show of cooperation. If you'd only let us know what you are looking for, we might be able to provide it for you, so we can avoid all of this unpleasantness. Southeastern is a reputable company that has done outstanding work in the community. It would be a shame to tarnish that reputation just because your young attorney wants to make a name for himself."

"As Mr. Eddy said, thank you for stopping by," the chief stated as he motioned toward his door. Ben was glad that his chief wasn't willing to budge or divulge any of the details about their investigation, no matter how small. They both knew they still had plenty of work ahead of them before they would be ready to take Southeastern or Delvers to court, but Ben and his team were committed to seeing this case through to the end.

Delvers shrugged and looked at Ms. Tammington, who raised her eyebrow in response. He wasn't quite able to hide the frustration from his features. The attorney leaned to the left and grasped her briefcase, then followed her client out of the office and down the hallway. The two whispered back and forth as they disappeared onto the elevator, their heads bent together as they plotted their next move.

Ben watched them go, then turned back to his chief once he was sure they were gone. "Well, that was a nasty pair."

The chief shook his head but smiled. "You doubt their sincerity? I'm shocked."

"I doubt every word they uttered. The last thing they want to do is be helpful."

The chief's smile faded. "Yet, they can be a dangerous adversary. They do have a lot of money and attorneys at their disposal, just like she said."

"Sure, but they are just fishing right now. They know we have Jordan, but they don't know we recovered the hard drive from the Sparks house. We'll find what we need to take them down. I'm sure of it."

"I hope so. As much as we were showering them with bravado, the last thing we need right now is a lawsuit to tie our hands and make our jobs even harder. Our resources are limited, just like any public agency."

Ben put his hands on his hips. "We're getting closer, Chief. We just need more time."

"You have some," the chief answered, "but don't think we can focus on this forever. If you don't find something soon, we'll need to move on to our other cases."

Ben nodded. "Message received, Chief. We'll step it up if we can." He exited the office and closed the door behind him, then went in search of Jordan to tell her about this latest development. They'd already been working as hard as humanly possible, but now he realized they no longer had time to wait for Bailey to find a way in to the mysterious hard drive. They had to pull out all the stops and follow even the most unlikely of leads.

NINE

"Can I get a caramel macchiato, please?" Jordan asked. She looked at the coffee shop's menu board once more and laid four dollars on the counter.

Ben was a few steps away, pretending to be another customer while watching the barista surreptitiously from the side of the counter. The wide eyes and narrow face were identical to those of the man in the photo on Ben's phone. His hair was a bit longer and had been pulled back into a ponytail, and he sported a well-groomed beard, but he was definitely the man they were looking for. According to the official records, their target was twenty-three years old, five-feet-eleven-inches high and weighed 174 pounds. All of that information matched, as well.

They had finally found the man they had been searching for and their hard work had paid off, but it hadn't been easy. Jordan and Bailey still hadn't discovered a way into the hard drive, so they had turned their attention to Samantha Peretti's murder. Chad Peretti, Samantha's son, had done an admirable job of disappearing into the woodwork after his mother had been killed, which had forced him to use a fake social security number to get a job. Ben was extremely thankful that Chad hadn't left Jacksonville. If he had, it would have been much harder to find him. With a little interoffice cooperation, however, Ben had been able to get a list of the workers in Duval County whose W-2s didn't match the name and social security numbers the Social Security Administration had on record. The administration didn't have a lot of manpower to investigate the discrepancies, but after failing to find Chad through other normal channels, Ben and Jordan had started searching using other resources, including federal databases they could access. Once they had limited the search parameters to match when Chad had disappeared and his age and gender, they had been able to narrow the list of possible suspects to five individuals. The man before them was number three on the list. They'd already seen the first two and been able to scratch them off this morning.

Ben eyed the exits of the coffee shop, then moved slightly and positioned himself between the counter and the dining room, effectively blocking off two of the ways out of the restaurant.

Chad glanced up at Jordan as he took her order. "Coming right up," he said jovially. He turned to make the drink, oblivious to Ben's perusal, then came back and put the steaming cup on the counter. "Three seventy-nine," he said as he took her money and punched in the amount at the cash register.

Ben didn't think that Chad would recognize Jordan, and he'd been right. In fact, the cashier was so engrossed in his work that he barely acknowledged the individual customers, except when he smiled and took their money. According to Jordan, the two had never met, even though Chad's mother had worked closely with her on the development of Mintax in the Southeastern lab. Samantha Peretti had kept a picture of Chad on her desk, however, and Jordan glanced at Ben and nodded, letting Ben know that they had indeed found the right man.

"Chad Peretti?" Ben asked.

The barista looked up quickly. "Ah, no. That's not my name. We don't have anyone named Chad working here. Are you sure you have the right store?"

Ben shook his head and took a step forward. The man was not a good liar. In fact, his face had paled at Ben's question and his hands had started shaking, even though he tried to hide it by wiping them again and again on his apron. Ben took another step closer to the counter, knowing that his big body created a formidable presence. "Yes, I'm sure, and you look amazingly like Mr. Peretti's driver's license photo."

The coffeehouse employee hesitated, then slowly lifted his head and looked Ben directly in the eye.

"I have one of those faces. You know—common. I look like a lot of people."

Ben shook his head and showed him his badge, then pocketed it. "I'm just not buying it. I'm Ben Graham with the Jacksonville Sheriff's Office, and this is Jordan Kendrick. She used to work with your mom. We have a few questions about Southeastern and the work they were doing at the lab. Can we go somewhere private to talk? We need your help."

"Sorry, I can't help you." Before the words were even completely out of his mouth, Chad turned and started running toward the kitchen, knocking people to the side as he did so and hitting one worker's arm who was carrying four cups of coffee in a brown box carrier. Coffee spewed all over the floor, across the bags of paper goods and made a truly sticky, steaming mess behind the counter.

Ben followed him immediately, his shoes gaining purchase despite the dark brown liquid that had coated the floor. He made a grab for the fleeing man but wasn't quite fast enough to touch more than just his apron strings before Chad escaped. He continued to chase him, slowed down by other workers who weren't aware of the drama unfolding and were surprised to see a customer in the employee-only area of the kitchen.

The barista pulled two racks of food over behind him, attempting to block Ben's path, and pans laden with pastries and scones flew off the shelves and contributed to the mélange. Chad finally made it to the rear door and hit it hard with his back, then whirled and disappeared out of the restaurant. Ben quickly pushed the racks aside and stepped over a couple of bags of paper goods, unfortunately knocking one female worker down as he did so in his haste to follow the man out of the building. He took the time to help her back to her feet and mutter a quick apology, then hurled himself after Chad Peretti, hitting the back door only moments behind the absconding barista.

There was no way Ben was going to let Chad Peretti escape. They had spent too much time tracking him down. Ben and Jordan didn't know what, if anything, he could add to the investigation, but right now, Chad was their only lead. So far, Bailey and the IT team still hadn't been able to break the encryption code on the hard drive they had found at the Sparks house, and they were hitting brick walls down every other avenue they had investigated. Jordan hadn't been able to find Chad on her own, but now that they had found him as a team, they were both hopeful he could give them something they could use. They knew Chad was probably antsy since he had gone to such lengths to disappear, but neither of them had expected him to run as soon as they revealed his true identity.

"Sherriff's Department! Stop!" Ben yelled, but Chad ignored the command and didn't even slow down as he left the coffee shop behind and sprinted under the raised Jacksonville Skyway train track. He ran up the stairs toward the train, jumped over the turnstile and headed into a sea of people that were waiting for the next monorail.

Ben jumped the turnstile as well, still about thirty feet behind his quarry. He pushed through the crowd, following Chad with his eyes by focusing on the brown apron and the dark ponytail. He wasn't exactly sure where Jordan had ended up, but he hoped she didn't stray too far away. Right now, all of his energy and focus had to be on catching Chad. If Samantha's son did manage to escape, they might not be able to find him again. He would probably go deeper into hiding and forget all about his job at the coffee shop, or leave Florida altogether, once and for all.

Like a world-class gymnast, Chad jumped on the handrail, steadied himself and pulled himself up on the metal roof that covered the train. Despite the noise from the commuters, Ben could hear Chad's feet pounding on the corrugated steel above him as he ran. Ben skidded to a stop and headed in the opposite direction as he followed the footsteps, once again pushing through the people and ignoring the bystanders who were yelling encouragement or recording him with their phones. When Chad reached the end of the roof, he locked eyes with Ben, who was leaning over the railing on the platform. For a moment they both froze, taking each other's measure. Then Chad jumped, grabbing the handrail of a nearby fire escape attached to a brick six-story high-rise. Ben heard the metal groan, but it held fast. He watched in amazement as Chad clung desperately to the metal railing and, after taking a breath, finally pulled himself up on the metal landing. The fugitive glanced down but must have decided not to chance jumping down twenty feet to the ground below. Instead, he started climbing while some of the rowdier bystanders cheered him on and recorded him with their phones.

Ben hit the handrail in frustration as he watched Chad try the windows on the landing. They were locked, but instead of trying to break one, he turned and headed up the metal staircase to the next level. Ben hadn't wanted the man to fall and get hurt, but Chad was doing an admirable job of evading him, and he was no longer sure he had a chance to stop him from escaping. He looked behind him and took in his surroundings once again, but he knew instinctively that if he took the time to go back down the stairs, there was no way he could catch Chad. The man simply had too much of a head start. He also doubted he could manage the same jump Chad had just successfully completed to the fire escape. From where he was standing, it was just too far away. He said a short prayer for safety, then swung his leg over the rail and started climbing down the side of the platform. There was a roof to the lower level about five feet below him, and he started swinging himself like a trapeze artist, hoping he wouldn't end up on the ground with a broken leg. His muscles strained, but he was instantly glad that he had worked so hard on his upper body strength. He was a big guy, and all of those chin-ups and pull-ups where he'd had to lift his entire body weight with his arms were paying off. He let the momentum carry him, and he let go at just the right time so he landed squarely on the roof of the substation below. He caught his balance and steadied himself, then ran a few steps and repeated the process, dropping himself down to the ground. A few moments later, he had pulled the fire escape ladder down and was climbing up after Chad.

The old brick building was six stories high, and he could still see Chad ascending above him. It looked like he was on the fifth floor, but it was hard to tell for sure. At least he was still on the fire escape and hadn't entered the building. Ben took the metal stairs two at a time, and made it to the fourth floor just in time to see Chad's legs disappearing over the edge of the roof.

Adrenaline surged as he continued the chase. His heart was pumping as he grabbed the handrail and swung up to the next level, again jumping the stairs as quickly as he could. He had to catch this guy. Jordan was counting on him. He couldn't take a chance that Chad would disappear without them learning everything he knew, if anything, about Southeastern and Mintax. He pushed himself harder until he made it to the roof, then bent over for a moment with his hands on his knees as he caught his breath. Quickly he straightened, his eyes darting around, looking for any sign of Chad. He arrived just in time to see the barista take a running start and jump right off the roof. Had the man just committed suicide to avoid being confronted? A cold sweat swept over Ben, despite the heat from the Jacksonville sun.

"No!" he yelled, making it across the roof in record time. He hit the edge of the concrete barrier and frantically looked below, afraid he was going to see Chad's broken body on the concrete. Instead, he saw Chad picking himself up off the roof of a nearby building, brushing the pebbles from his hands. Chad looked frantically behind him, and once again, their eyes met.

The buildings were about eight feet apart, and the building where Chad had landed was one floor lower than where Ben stood. Unlike the fire escape maneuver, this was a jump Ben was confident he could make. He took several steps back, then got a running start and jumped after Chad. The younger man had anticipated what Ben was going to do and had already started running away from him. As Ben landed and skidded on the rocks, Chad sprinted toward the door on the roof, pulled on the knob and disappeared as the door closed slowly behind him.

Ben steadied himself and continued the chase, heading for the stairwell. He threw the door open and followed Chad down the stairs. He could hear the man below, his feet pounding against the steps, and as he turned to the next landing, he caught a glimpse of Chad's brown apron. The next thing he heard was the door below opening and closing as the barista left the building. Ben's heart was beating like a bass drum as he made it to the bottom and pushed through the door, continuing the chase. He caught a glimpse of his target about thirty feet away, took a deep breath and raced after him into a nearby park.

An older couple was walking arm in arm down the sidewalk that ran through the middle of the park, and Ben was instantly thankful that Chad took the time to go around them instead of plowing into them and causing serious damage. The man might have been frantic and scared, but he hadn't forgotten his humanity during the chase. A large leashed dog barked at the fleeing man, and Chad carefully avoided the animal and owner as well, all of which cost him precious time. He glanced behind him, and his eyes grew large as he saw how close Ben was to catching him. He tried to speed up, but he was breathing hard and struggling, apparently not used to all of the physical exertion the chase was causing.

Ben caught him in a flying tackle and brought him to the ground on the last patch of grass available before they reached the concrete street that bordered the park. Chad struggled, trying to free himself, but he was no match for Ben, who had wrestled in both high school and college and knew exactly how to pin a man down. With just a few quick moves, Ben had the barista's arms trapped and pinned tightly against his head. He cuffed him, even as the man struggled to catch his breath after the wind had been knocked out of him when he'd hit the ground. Ben hadn't wanted to arrest the man, only ask him some questions, but now he had to make sure Samantha's son wasn't going to strike out or disappear again before they discovered what he knew about Southeastern. Fleeing was almost always a sign of guilt. Was Chad guilty of something beyond working under the table with a false name and trying to survive?

"You can't arrest me!" Chad spat, his motions desperate as he jerked against the cuffs. "I haven't broken any laws. And you know as well as I do that if Southeastern finds me, they'll kill me."

Ben led him over to a nearby bench and forced him to sit. Chad did so awkwardly, his hands secured behind him. The professional well-groomed man they had first encountered had disappeared, and a frantic, desperate man was now in his place. If Ben remembered correctly, Chad recently graduated with a business degree from the University of North Florida, right here in Jacksonville. This was a smart, capable man before him, but the look on his face was haunted and gaunt, and the anger was evident, as well as the fear that was stretched across his features.

"Last I heard, using a false social security number was frowned upon. But that's not why we're here. It is interesting that you would run at the mere mention of Southeastern. We need to have a conversation." Ben fisted his hands on his hips. "We just want to talk."

"We?" Chad said, looking around suspiciously. "All I see is you."

Ben looked around for a moment, then motioned toward Jordan once he spotted her running toward them. He was relieved that she had been able to figure out where they had ended up, despite the chase. He noted that she had stopped to calm the older couple for a moment before heading in their direction. The pair seemed very disturbed by the flying tackle and arrest they had just seen, but with a smile and a pat on the lady's back, Jordan was able to send them on their way. She also waved at the dog owner and assured the other onlookers that all was well and they should go on about their business. By the time she reached Ben's side, most of the audience had already dispersed.

He took a moment and really looked at Jordan. Her face was flushed from her own exertion, but in his mind, she had never looked lovelier. She was wearing khaki slacks and a navy blouse that delightfully accentuated her curves. Her cheeks were pink, her eyes were shining, and he could see that for the first time in quite a while she was feeling safe and had hope for the future. An ache filled his heart as he yearned for the past. They had been so happy before she had disappeared. They'd spent hours planning their future, laughing on the beach, and just enjoying each other's company. Could he ever regain that trust and love that had been so strong between them, or was their relationship permanently broken? Ever since her return, his mind had gone back and forth, considering the possibilities. At this point, he wasn't sure what he wanted. He loved her and always would, but could he trust her? He asked God for guidance, then quickly tamped down his roaming thoughts and focused on the job in front of him. Now wasn't the time to start sorting through his feelings about Jordan.

Jordan smiled at Ben, a look of relief evident across her features, and he was instantly glad that she couldn't read his thoughts. She lightly touched his shoulder, unaware of the turmoil raging in his core. "Wow! I don't know how you did it, but I'm so glad you got him. For a minute there, I thought I was watching some crazy new show like *The Ninja Warriors Live from Jacksonville*." Ben glanced away to hide the pleasure he felt at her compliment. He took a step back, letting Jordan take the lead with questioning Chad. He knew instinctively that she would get more out of him with her questions that he would. He had to admit, they made a pretty good team.

Jordan turned to Chad and raised an eyebrow. "Are you okay?"

Chad glared at her, so she just pushed on. "Look, Chad, I'm sorry we had to chase you down like this, but we really needed to talk to you. I'm Jordan Kendrick. I used to work with your mother at Southeastern, and I've been looking for you for a long time." She pointed at Ben. "This is Ben Graham, and he's a deputy with the Sheriff's Office, like he said earlier. He's helping me investigate Southeastern and a drug we were working on called Mintax. We're not trying to hurt you, and we're not going to tell Southeastern or anybody else where we found you. We understand more than most how dangerous Southeastern can be. We just need answers so we can stop them before they hurt somebody else. Can we go somewhere and talk?"

Chad shook his head vigorously. "I don't want to talk to you, and I can't talk about them. If I do, they'll kill me just like they killed my mom."

Jordan took a step forward, adding as much conviction as she could to her voice. "Chad, this is your chance to get justice." Somehow, she had to convince him to talk to them. Samantha's son could have the key to solving this entire case.

He looked Jordan in the eye. "My mother mentioned you. I thought you were dead, too. I heard something about a boating accident. You know they killed Sparks, right?"

"We know he's dead," Ben confirmed. "As well as his wife. His death was initially ruled an accident, but we're reinvestigating the deaths of both your mom and Mr. Sparks to find out for sure what really happened."

"Please talk to us," Jordan pleaded. "We can't let them get away with what they're doing. You're one of the few people who might really know what happened."

"I can't," Chad repeated, his tone frantic. "If I do, they'll kill me for sure. Why do you think I was hiding my true identity?" He tried to stand, but Ben pushed him back down with a hand on his shoulder.

"You're not going anywhere," he said quietly, but with authority in his voice. "Not until we get some answers."

TEN

Thirty minutes later, the three of them were back in the coffee shop, meeting in the manager's office, the door closed for privacy. Chad's handcuffs had been removed, but he still hadn't agreed to talk to them. He sat in the corner, pressed against the wall, and Jordan was sure that if it were possible, he would have found a way to melt into the Sheetrock. There was no way for him to look more uncomfortable.

Even so, Jordan had done all she could to smooth things over with the coffee shop manager after Chad's flight from the store. She had explained to the lady that Chad was helping them with an important case, but that he had unfortunately mistaken them for people that were trying to hurt him. She'd also given the manager a hundred dollars to help cover the cost of the ruined pastries that had hit the floor during the chase. The manager had taken one look at Ben's badge and offered them the office to use with no questions asked, and also promised to keep the day's events private. She had even promised that Chad's flight and the mess he'd made in the back wouldn't affect his job.

This news, however, had done little to change Chad's mind about talking to them. Jordan softened her voice and continued in her quest to persuade him to help. "Look, Chad, I know you're scared, but we've reached an impasse and we need your help." She grasped his arm and squeezed it, but he quickly pulled it away from her. "*I* need your help." She sat back, hoping he would raise his head and look her in the eye. He didn't respond, but she pushed forward anyway, trying a different tact. "Did you know your mom kept a picture of you on her desk?" She waited, and eventually he glanced up at her.

"Yeah."

Jordan pressed on. "She was really proud of you. And when you graduated from UNF, you would have thought that the powers that be had declared it a national holiday. She went around the whole office passing out UNF stickers and cupcakes to everyone she came across in the lab. It was a really big day for her." She leaned in. "Did you know she did that?"

Chad shook his head, still maintaining his silence.

"She told me once that you were the best thing that ever happened to her. She was hoping you were going to go for your master's degree, but if not, that was okay, too. She was always saying you were smart and talented and would succeed at anything you tried." Jordan shifted, letting those words hang there for a moment. "I think the same thing you do. I think someone at Southeastern had her killed because she knew too much about a drug they were developing called Mintax. Your mom and I worked very closely together at the lab. I know she had collected data about Mintax, and right now, we need to find anything we can that proves what the drug can do and how it hurt people during the trials. We don't have access to Southeastern's computers yet, but we do know they tried to destroy everything they could about Mintax and the drug trials. We're hoping your mom might have held on to something that shows the details about the drug's development. We're grasping at straws here, but Southeastern has to be stopped before they hurt anybody else." Her voice was firm, but she still kept her tone low and soothing. "And, they need to be held responsible for killing your mom."

Ben had been standing behind Jordan, but now he sat on the edge of the manager's desk. He had also softened his voice, and Jordan noticed he had tried to stay in the background and appear as nonthreatening as possible. "Try to remember anything you can about what your mom might have said or done about the drug before her death," he asked. "Please. Even if you don't think it's important, it might be crucial to our case. Also, anything you still have from Southeastern might be useful—notes, computer files, records of any kind."

Chad twisted the apron fabric in his hands, tighter and tighter. Finally, he spoke. "They'll kill me. I know they killed my mom. If I say anything at all, they'll kill me, too. I can't help you."

"Are you saying you want to spend the rest of your life in hiding, living under an assumed name? That's what will happen if we can't prove our case. We have to stop them. And for your mom's sake, we have to show that they were responsible! The only way to end this is to help us," Jordan pleaded.

"Look," Ben said quietly. "Let's start out by just talking about your mom. Did you see her the day she died?"

Chad finally looked up at that question. "Yes, I was still living at home. It was a Thursday. I remember we ate breakfast together. We had pancakes."

Jordan tried not to smile as jubilation filled her. He was talking! Now, hopefully, they would get somewhere. "Did she say or do anything out of the ordinary?" she asked.

"No. It was just like any other day."

Ben shifted. "How about a week or so before she died. Did you see anyone suspicious around your house? Anyone or anything that seemed out of place?"

Chad looked up as if trying to remember, but finally shook his head. "No. Nothing out of the ordinary."

"Did you see anything that made you suspect something might be wrong?"

Chad shrugged. "Not really. She did seem a bit more stressed than normal, but when I asked her about it, she just said she was having some problems at work, but that the issues would all sort themselves out soon enough. I was actually going to ride with her into the city that morning, but she had to leave early because she had an appointment with someone. If I had gone with her, I would have died, too."

"That appointment was with me," Jordan confirmed. "We were going to talk about Jeremy Sparks's death and what was going on with the Mintax drug trials. I think somehow Southeastern found out about our plans. I also think the Sparkses and your mom were all killed to keep them quiet so the scandal surrounding the drug didn't come out."

"Well, you're still here," he said bitterly as he glared at her. "I guess that boating accident didn't really happen."

Jordan shook her head. "You don't understand. When I heard about your mom, I went straight to the authorities. I ended up testifying against Southeastern and then entering the federal witness protection program. But the case against Southeastern went south and they only got a slap on the wrist for what they did. Even so, Southeastern still sent somebody to kill me, and they very nearly succeeded. That's why I'm back in Florida now, trying to make this right. I'm still not safe, but I'm doing what I can to bring what Southeastern did to light, so they can be held responsible for their crimes. I want them to pay for your mother's death, and I want to stop them before they hurt anybody else." Jordan paused and leaned closer so that she could catch his eye and hold his gaze. "You must know something, right? Otherwise, you wouldn't have gone to such lengths to hide yourself from Southeastern. Please tell us what you know."

Chad grimaced, and Jordan could see the muscles working in his jaw as he gritted his teeth. A moment passed. Then another. He tried to look away but she moved slightly, and a few moments later, he was trapped by her eyes once again. Finally, he sighed.

"I don't know a lot about what was actually happening at Southeastern. My mom didn't talk about it much, or at least she didn't talk to me about it. But before my mother died, she gave me a notebook full of handwritten notes and documents. I'm no scientist, but I do know it's filled with chemical formulas. She told me I had to keep it safe at all costs."

"Where is that notebook?" Jordan asked, struggling to keep her voice even and controlled, despite the excitement that immediately began coursing through her veins.

Chad's mouth tightened. "I can't give it to you. That notebook is my only bargaining chip. If Southeastern ever finds me, I can trade it for my life."

"Southeastern doesn't like loose ends," Jordan answered, her tone now matter-of-fact. "If they find out it exists, they'll take the notebook. Then they'll kill you for sure—just to make sure you're no longer a threat. Afterward, they'll destroy the notebook to protect themselves."

Chad considered her words. Jordan could actually see him sorting through his options by the look on his face. She decided to put all of her cards on the table.

"Southeastern has to be stopped, Chad," she said forcefully. "Your mom and I helped develop a dangerous drug that hurts people, but Southeastern has either hidden or destroyed all of the evidence. The Feds slapped the CEO and the company with a few fines, but those are the only consequences they've experienced, despite all the people they hurt. Your mom was killed so they could get away with their crimes, and I had to go into WITSEC just to stay alive. We can't let them get away with it. That notebook she gave you could be the key to stopping them once and for all. It might be able to help us prove what Southeastern did so we can break this case wide open. The Sheriff's Office has opened their own investigation, and we have a prosecutor ready to go as soon as we can bring him the proof he needs to put the case together."

Chad pulled his lips into a thin line. She could still see the fear in his features, but he had made his decision. "It's in my safe-deposit box at First Federal Bank downtown—box 134." He pulled a chain from around his neck that had a key dangling from the end. He removed the key and put it on the desk. "It's all yours."

Jordan accepted the key and looked back at Ben, who gave her a warm smile. Finally, they had a solid lead. She tried to stay focused on the case, but the look in his eyes did funny things to her insides. Did Ben still have any feelings beyond friendship for her? How could he, after all that she had done? It was impossible. Still, the attraction and love for him that she had felt hadn't faded, and an ache of regret and loss tightened in her chest.

She turned away, unhappy with where her thoughts had strayed. She said a short but heartfelt prayer of thanks for God's help in finding Chad, and for convincing him to aid in their quest to stop Southeastern. She fervently hoped that the notebook would contain the information they needed to finally stop Southeastern for good.

About thirty minutes later, Ben and Jordan had driven over to the bank that Chad had used to store the notebook, parked and entered the building. Ben had already talked to both Eddy, the state attorney and his supervisor at the Sheriff's Office to let them know what they had discovered. Eddy had immediately scheduled an appointment to meet with them as soon as they could retrieve the notebook and Jordan had a chance to digest the contents. If the book contained what they anticipated, Eddy was hopeful that they might be able to get subpoenas for Southeastern's records as early as tomorrow.

The bank employee slid the security deposit box out of the slot, put it on the table in the small privacy area and pulled the curtain closed so Ben and Jordan could open the box without prying eyes watching their progress.

Ben kept his hands on his belt and his stance alert as Jordan opened the box. He didn't expect trouble, but it paid to be cautious. Right on top, she found a two-inch-deep three-ring notebook. It was a simple black binder with no identifying cover, but the inside was filled with documents, notes and even a manila envelope stashed in the front pocket. Jordan thumbed through the documents, giving them a cursory view as she went from page to page. Her entire face lit up as she pulled out the envelope and poured the contents into her hand. Ten small blue pills rolled out. She glanced up at his face and smiled, and the look of utter happiness made his heart flutter. She was glowing. There was no other word for it.

"Is that Mintax?" he asked.

She nodded. "It sure is. I can't believe she even saved samples. With these and her notes… We won't have any trouble proving what Mintax did to those homeless people in the trials. We might even be able to somehow trace them to Sparks's death. I'm convinced they killed him with Mintax. If Eddy can get us a copy of his autopsy based on this new evidence, we might be able to find the proof we need." She returned the pills to the envelope, sealed the top and put it back in the notebook. "Thank you, Ben. I never would have been able to find this without you."

She took a step forward as if she was going to hug him, but then stopped herself as if unsure. Ben did nothing to encourage her. He suddenly felt awkward himself, and his own feelings were a jumbled mess inside his heart. Did he want Jordan to hug him, to touch him? Did he want to resume his relationship with her? He still loved her. He knew that. But was love enough?

By disappearing on her own without a word, Jordan had destroyed Ben's trust in her. Could he continue to love her without trusting her? He didn't think so—the insecurity would eat him up from the inside out. Every time she was out of his sight, he would have those lingering doubts. Would she disappear again if the going got tough? Would she even let him help her with her problems, or would she always try to solve them by herself? He wasn't sure how to get past the betrayal he felt. He understood her reasons for her actions, but understanding didn't erase the giant ball of hurt he felt whenever he remembered what she had done.

He was still lost in thought as he and Jordan left the bank and returned to his car in the parking lot. They headed back to Ben's office. Jordan needed time to study the notebook in a safe, quiet place and then they could meet with the team and discuss their plans about moving forward, depending on what Jordan discovered. Afterward, they would head over to talk to Eddy and work on their legal strategy.

Ben changed lanes and noticed a black SUV that was about forty feet back followed suit. His senses immediately went on high alert. He couldn't see the driver, but there seemed to be only one person in the vehicle. He stopped at a red light, his eyes on the SUV and the surrounding cars, as well.

"Is there a problem?" Jordan asked as she looked up from the notebook.

"I don't know yet. We might have picked up a tail." The light turned green, and Ben punched the gas, speeding in front of the car in the right lane of the four-lane road and making a quick turn onto the side street. He looked in his rearview mirror and wasn't surprised to see the black SUV mirror his actions. "Yes, we're being followed alright." He reached for his phone and quickly called it in, then changed lanes again, hoping to put as much space as possible between them and their pursuer. As he drove, he tried once again to get a look at the driver, but he didn't make much progress. He could tell it was a white man wearing a baseball cap and sunglasses, but that was about as close of a description as he could make out while he was driving.

"Jordan, take a look at that black SUV that's following us and see if you can recognize the driver. Also, let me know if you see anyone else in the vehicle."

"Will do," she answered as she turned and craned her neck to get a better look.

Ben sped around a white pickup truck, then hit the accelerator to make it through a light as it turned red. He quickly located the SUV behind him and was shocked to see it follow them through the intersection, despite narrowly missing a minivan and being clipped in the rear driver's side bumper by a two-door sports car. The SUV fishtailed but continued its pursuit and was gaining fast, despite Ben's maneuvers.

Ben's tires squealed as his sedan swerved into the left lane and he passed three new cars, narrowly missing them as he rocketed forward. He saw smoke from the road and smelled the burning rubber from his tires, but he ignored both as he focused on their escape. He didn't know for sure why they were being chased, but he had a good idea. The notebook in Jordan's hands was probably the key to bringing Southeastern down. If the pharmaceutical company had indeed already killed to keep their secrets, taking out two more people would hardly make a difference in the grand scheme of things. He imagined Southeastern had been following Jordan ever since she had arrived at his door, and keeping them both under surveillance despite his attempts to ensure she was safely hidden away. They had probably just been waiting to see what, if anything, they discovered with their investigation. If they had been following them, it wouldn't have been too hard for them to put two and two together and realize what they had just retrieved from the safe-deposit box. He would have to check his car later, if they survived this encounter, to see if he could find a GPS or other tracker that had been hidden on his car.

The SUV driver was good. He was sticking to them like glue, and the SUV had both the size and weight advantage. Even though Ben's sedan was built to law enforcement specs, the SUV was a bigger vehicle with a stronger engine. The driver hadn't tried to shoot at them, but he was still gaining on them quickly, and they were almost to the Buckman Bridge. A seed of worry started to grow in Ben's chest. Once they were on the bridge, there was no way to make a U-turn or pull onto a side street to escape their pursuer. They would be well and truly stuck. Ben looked for a way to keep from driving toward the bridge, but it was too late—he had already passed all of the available exits, and there was no other safe way to get off the roadway. He glanced in his rearview mirror once again and grimaced as the SUV hit them hard from behind.

Jordan shrieked and gripped the armrests tightly as she pressed against the seat.

"Hold on!" Ben yelled, as he swerved once again, this time going around a large semitrailer truck as he changed lanes. A red car in front of them slowed dramatically, and Ben suddenly had to spin the wheel and speed around it, narrowly missing the red car's rear fender as he surged ahead. A silver pickup truck slowed in front of them and he twisted the wheel back to the right, once again barely avoiding the other vehicle. He was thankful that there were eight lanes of traffic, four going each direction, with somewhat lighter traffic than usual. The black SUV was only a few feet behind, following each of his maneuvers with ease. *Was the driver a former NASCAR racer?* he wondered fleetingly. The guy's driving skills were amazing. There didn't seem any way to shake him off their tail, and Ben began to wonder if they would even make it across the river.

A few seconds later, they were driving on the Buckman Bridge. The black SUV pulled up alongside Ben and Jordan screamed again as the SUV scraped against their sedan, pushing it to the right. Ben fought against the wheel but couldn't keep them from moving over to the right lane, barely missing a tow truck as they did so. The right front fender of his car hit the concrete barrier and they were suddenly sandwiched between the SUV and the guardrail. The metal whined and screeched as it crinkled from the abuse, and Ben watched helplessly as the tow truck behind them hit the side as well before spinning into traffic. He heard tires squealing and several loud booms as cars crashed behind them, but he had to stay focused on the SUV, which had finally been forced to pull away before it could push them even farther into the barrier wall. Both sides of their car were now demolished from the SUV's actions, but thankfully, the car was still drivable.

Unexpectedly, the SUV was back in the left lane next to them again, just as they were passing the apex of the bridge. They traveled another fifty feet or so without incident. Then suddenly the passenger's front side of the SUV struck the driver's side of their sedan with a crunch and both vehicles spun out of control. Their car careened toward the concrete barrier wall once again, but this time the momentum made it flip over and the vehicle skidded for several yards on the roof before it came to rest dangerously balanced on the concrete partition, halfway over the concrete guardrail and leaning precariously toward the St. Johns River below.

ELEVEN

Jordan couldn't seem to let go of the seat belt, even though her fingers were straining from the deathlike grip she had on the fabric. Once the car finally stopped moving, she tried to gather her bearings, but she was afraid to move. She was upside down and disoriented, but held precariously in her seat with the seat belt that was biting into her skin. The good news was she was alive, but for how long? She shifted slightly and felt the car tilt underneath her. Was the vehicle going to topple into the water below? She looked toward the windshield and could see the blue ripples of the St. Johns River churning beneath her. The smells of fish, automotive grease and burned rubber warred for supremacy, and the acrid smells choked in her throat. To make matters worse, Samantha Peretti's notebook had flown out of her hands at impact, and she wasn't quite sure what had happened to it. She couldn't see it, and she desperately wanted to twist around and look for it. She was afraid that if she did, however, she would send the car careening into the river.

She looked quickly over at Ben, who was similarly held in place by his seat belt. He had several small cuts on his face and arms from the flying glass, but his brown eyes were open and alert, and he looked otherwise unharmed.

"Are you okay?" she asked softly. She was surprised at the huskiness of her own voice. She'd done enough screaming during the car chase to last her a lifetime, and her heart was still pounding against her chest and felt like it was about to burst. Would the fear never end? Her life seemed like a roller coaster that never pulled into the station to end the ride. She could still feel the adrenaline pumping through her veins.

"I'm okay," he responded with a groan. "I'm a bit sore, but right now, I'm just happy we're both alive. How are you doing?"

"I'll make it. I don't have any serious injuries. Yet." She took several deep breathes, hoping to calm her shredded nerves. She tried to brush the hair out of her eyes but stopped suddenly as the motion caused the car to rock.

"Don't move," Ben intoned, his lips drawn into a thin line. "We're going to be fine, but I think our car is just barely balanced on the concrete guardrail. We've got to wait for help to arrive so they can stabilize the car before we try to get out." He very cautiously moved his arm toward the steering wheel and turned the car's motor off.

"You've got a lot of small cuts from the glass," she said softly. "Are you sure you're not dizzy or bleeding anywhere else?"

He gingerly brushed some of the glass from his hair. "I don't think so."

The side-curtain air bags had both deployed and were basically filling the space where the door windows had been. The air bag fabric blocked the view, but they could still hear traffic noises from outside. Jordan wanted to push them away so she could see if anyone had stopped to help, but she was afraid to move.

"What do you think happened to the black SUV that was chasing us?" she asked, hoping that their pursuer had chosen to flee instead of sticking around to finish the job. Surely, other drivers had realized what had happened and reported the assault. If nothing else, she hoped one of the drivers had managed to call 911 so the first responders could rush to the scene and help them before their car careened off the bridge. She hadn't gotten a good look at the driver that had caused the accident, but if they could somehow figure out who had attacked them, maybe they could link him to Southeastern, as well. One could hope, even when the situation was as dire as the one they found themselves in right now.

She said a quick prayer of thankfulness that they had both survived and were relatively unharmed, then turned her focus back to the missing notebook.

"Do you see Samantha's notebook?" Jordan asked. "It flew out of my hands when we crashed, but I can't see where it landed. We can't let it fall into the river."

She suddenly heard a ripping sound, and she saw a knife sawing through the air bag by her door. A few seconds later, the airbag was mostly removed and flapping harmlessly against the door frame from where it hung by a small remaining section near the windshield. She felt the heat from the asphalt enter the car through the broken passenger door with a whoosh. She couldn't see who had cut away the thin nylon fabric, but she heard a small laugh. "So, you survived the crash," a deep male voice she didn't recognize said from behind her. "Don't worry. I'll take care of that notebook for you."

She startled but dared not move to turn around and see who had spoken. It had to be the driver of the SUV who had gotten out of his vehicle and was now crouching down behind the passenger's side back door. She could see his shadow, but not the man himself. Although the window glass had shattered upon impact, she guessed that there were still pieces of it that were intact around the window frame. She heard him bat against it, breaking more of the glass as he made the opening wider before he reached inside the car.

The car tilted as a result of his actions, and Jordan couldn't help herself. She screamed and gripped the armrests so tightly her fingers started hurting and turning white once again.

"Take the notebook," Ben said, his voice filled with both helplessness and hostility. "Just please don't push the car over the railing. Take it and go."

Jordan quickly looked over at Ben, her eyes wide. He could definitely see the interloper more clearly from his seat than she could, but why was he offering up the notebook? She couldn't lose it. She just couldn't—especially now since they finally had their hands on the proof they were seeking. She opened her mouth to protest but felt Ben's hand give her arm a tender squeeze. She glanced up and met his eyes, seeing the gentle plea there—*Trust me. I know what I'm doing.* She nodded and clamped her lips together, still gripping the armrests. Ben understood the significance of the notebook. She knew he would do what he could to save it, and she also knew that whatever the notebook contained, it wasn't worth their lives.

Their attacker reached in and closed the open notebook, which was resting on the ceiling of the overturned vehicle, before pulling it out the window and brushing off the bits of broken glass and debris that had collected on the cover. He wasn't wearing sunglasses any longer, and Ben could see a coldness that filled the man's dark brown eyes. The man had no remorse or conscience. Even though his hair was covered with a Jaguars cap, Ben thought the assailant looked remarkably like the same man that had attacked him only a couple of days before in his own home. He even thought he saw the same small scar under the man's left eye. He had no doubt that a company the size of Southeastern could have several men such as this mercenary on their payroll. He wondered fleetingly if he was also looking at the man who had murdered Jeremy Sparks and his wife, along with Samantha Peretti.

"Thanks for this," the man said in a gruff tone. "We've been looking for it for quite a while." He smiled, but there was no mirth in his expression. He put his hand on the frame of the car. "You've caused me all sorts of trouble. I hope you can swim."

"Don't do it," Ben said quickly. "You have what you need. You don't need to kill us."

"Ah, but if I don't, you will continue to be a problem. Besides, what's two more? As I said, I hope you can swim." He smiled malevolently again, then stood. Ben could see the man's legs as he circled the car, and he grabbed Jordan's hand and squeezed it, imagining that the man was studying the best way to cause the most damage. He knew their time for talking was short.

"Don't be afraid," Ben said quickly and softly, hoping their enemy couldn't hear him. "We can do this. Okay? Hold on to your seat belt as we fall, just like you're doing, and pull up your feet so your ankles don't get hurt." He felt the car tip and rushed on with his instructions. "That seat belt is going to save your life. From this angle, the car will probably hit the water upside down. Once it does, the front air bags will deploy. After that happens, just shove yours out of the way, okay? Then you're going to have to push yourself against the roof of the car to ease the tension before you try to get out of your seat belt. If the car doesn't flip over, then as soon as we hit, just go straight to work on getting out of that belt." He caught her eyes and held them, making sure he had her full attention. "Since the windows are broken, the car will fill up really quickly with water, but there will be a minute or so before it goes under and sinks. Keep your seat belt on until we hit, and if we're upside down, then just push against the roof and unfasten it as fast as you can. Then swim out of your window, okay? If you get disoriented, look for air bubbles or head toward the light. That river is pretty murky, but I don't think it's very deep. The bubbles and the light will show you the way up to the surface. Got it?"

Her eyes were filled with fear as they both felt the

car tilt even more precariously. The man was apparently pushing against the frame, and they all knew the car needed very little pressure to go over the edge. Ben heard metal scraping against the concrete, and the car whined like a badly played French horn. Jordan screamed again, but Ben kept talking, his tone low and steady, even as the car moved.

"Once we're in the water, don't worry about me. Remember, push against the roof before trying to release your seat belt. Just get yourself out of the car, and swim toward the surface. Got it?"

"What about you?" she asked, her voice frantic.

"Worry about you," he repeated. "Just remember—get out of your seat belt first, then swim to the surface. I'll be waiting for you."

The metal groaned, and they could hear it bending and straining against the pull of gravity. Suddenly the car tilted even farther toward the water, and the metal whined once more before the entire car careened toward the St. Johns River below. It felt as if they were on a roller coaster that had just started moving, and the car seemed to be falling in slow motion at an incredibly sluggish rate. In fact, Ben actually noticed the sky and land through the windshield and even recognized a seagull flying by before the car hit the water. It was an odd yet chilling feeling that sent a fission of anxiety down his spine.

With a loud crash, the front of the car hit the water, as if the vehicle had just hit a wall of concrete in a head-on collision. The front air bags instantly inflated upon impact, and the car bobbed a couple of times before flipping upside down once again. Once the car settled, it took Ben a moment or two to regain his bearings, and he was actually stunned at how fast the car was sinking. Water rushed in through the broken windows, and Ben quickly pushed the air bag away from his chest. He looked for Jordan to make sure she was okay. He was relieved to see she was conscious, and their eyes met for a brief moment before they both started to work on unhooking their seat belts. Jordan's arms flailed, and she struggled with the belt as her eyes grew wide and filled with panic.

"I can't get the seat belt off!" she said frantically. "It's stuck!" Water was already in their hair and continuing to rise at a rapid rate. The murky water bubbled around them and seeped into every crevice of the car.

Ben braced himself against the car frame to ease the tension on his own seat belt and quickly pushed the button to release it. With one final tug, he was free. He continued to push against the frame as he maneuvered himself so that his feet were on the ceiling of the car and he was crouching upright. He was instantly glad once again that all those hours he had spent working on his upper body strength were finally paying off. He leaned over so he could get a better grasp of Jordan's seat belt trouble. She was growing more terrified by the moment and her arms thrashed in desperation as she tugged against the belt. He tried his best to avoid her fists as he quickly assessed what needed to be done.

"Pull yourself up against the frame and try to keep your head above the water," he yelled, hoping to get her attention over the rising panic she was exhibiting.

He wasn't even sure she understood him in her current state. He reached across her body for the cam-lock belt buckle and pressed against the button, but the belt mechanism simply wouldn't release the tongue. Suddenly, an idea hit him and he reached into his pocket. Upon graduation from the police academy, his father had gifted him a three-inch engraved Spyderco Police Model folding knife. He kept it with him always as a keepsake, never really expecting to use it, but incredibly thankful that he had it with him today. He flipped it open and started sawing at the seat belt webbing that stretched across her waist. He glanced up into Jordan's face and saw the fear mirrored back at him as the water started to cover her mouth. She sputtered and choked, even as he saw her strong determination to survive in her eyes. His own adrenaline surged in response.

With one final tug, the belt separated, and he tried to catch her body and ease her out of the strap that was holding her to the seat. The water had risen past her head by now, and her flailing had increased somewhat as she had struggled just to find air to breathe. He understood her panic. The body had a natural instinct to protect itself against drowning, and Jordan's instinct was to push against him and find air regardless of the cost, just like a panicked swimmer. That inner voice didn't recognize reason or the help that Ben was trying to provide, and the best thing he could do now was get out of her way. He pushed himself back, giving her some space to flip her body right-side up and get her legs underneath her.

The air bag that the assailant had ripped was waving in the water and kept getting in his way as he tried to open the passenger's side door. It was impossible. The door was stuck. Time might have been moving in slow motion during their fall, but it was now speeding by at an incredible rate. He knew he only had moments before the entire car was underwater. He finally gave up on the passenger's side door and pushed against his own driver's side door. It opened slowly but was hampered by his own curtain-side air bag. He made short work of the nylon fabric with his knife and saw enough space to pull himself through. He turned back to Jordan and stretched out his hand. She had righted herself and found a small pocket of air, and she was gulping and sputtering.

He found his own pocket of air and inhaled a deep breath, then called to her. "Jordan, come with me. I found a way out." She glanced at him, but in her current state of fear, he imagined his voice barely registered. The taste of oxygen made her more frantic instead of calming her, and when he reached for her, she pushed against him, fighting his efforts without really understanding that he was trying to help.

The car continued to fill with water, and Ben took in a large lungful of air from the last little available pocket before the vehicle was completely inundated. He pulled Jordan's body against his own and wrapped one strong arm around her torso. She wrestled against him, but he held her fast. Then he used every ounce of strength he had to pull himself and Jordan out through the driver's side door. Once their upper bodies were out, he continued to push against the car with his legs until both of them were completely free of the car. As he verified that they had both cleared the metal, he pushed against the car frame one last time and saw it slowly sink beneath them. Then he turned and headed toward the surface with Jordan securely in his arms.

Jordan had stopped fighting him.

Ben's heartbeat accelerated. She was drowning! He couldn't lose her now. The need for air pressed heavily within his own chest, and he turned his face upward, heading toward the light above him and following the air bubbles that escaped from his nose. He kicked with all of his strength and swam with one arm while pulling Jordan with his other. His lungs burned, and his entire chest started to ache as he slowly propelled both himself and Jordan upward toward the light. Could he make it to the surface in time and still save Jordan, or was he too late?

TWELVE

A few seconds later, Ben's head broke through the water, and he sucked in a great gulp of air. Thankfully, the water in the river was only about twenty feet deep, and it hadn't taken him long to reach the surface. Hurriedly, he turned his attention to Jordan. She wasn't breathing. He treaded water for a moment, assessing their situation. They were still a good distance from the nearest piling, and he didn't want to wait to try helping her.

He turned her body so they were now face-to-face and checked her airway to make sure it was clear of debris. The waves weren't horrible, but he kept an eye on them, making sure the rising swells didn't cover Jordan's face. He pulled gently on the corner of her mouth, allowing it to drain, then hooked his free arm over Jordan's arm and placed his hand against the back of her neck, supporting it while he tilted her head. With his other hand, he pinched her nose and sealed it, moving her head slightly to open the airway. He gave her two quick rescue breaths.

Nothing happened.

"Dear, God, please help me!" he prayed frantically. He pressed the heel of his hand to her forehead, tilting it back a bit farther to make sure her airway was open and pinched her nostrils closed one more time. Then he turned her body toward him and gave Jordan four quick rescue breaths.

Again, nothing happened.

Then suddenly she sputtered, and water poured from her mouth. He tilted her head a bit to help the water drain and continued to hold her well above the water as she revived. She coughed, and more water dribbled out of her mouth and nose. Ben treaded water continuously, keeping them both supported as Jordan slowly recovered and started breathing on her own.

"You're going to be okay," he soothed. He continued to whisper words of encouragement in her ear as he brushed her hair gently away from her face. Relief swamped over him. She was alive! For the second time in his life, he had almost lost her. He pulled her close, enjoying the feel of her in his arms. For a moment, he just reveled in the touch, thankful that God had saved them from a watery grave. Then he slowly started swimming toward the nearest piling that had rocks around the base, listening carefully to her breathing as he did so. He traveled headfirst with Jordan held closely by his side, and the forward momentum helped keep water out of her face. They moved slowly, but at this point, Ben was more concerned about Jordan's safety than he was about speed. She continued to take in huge gulps of air as he swam, but the rest of her body had relaxed and wasn't fighting him as he moved effortlessly through the water.

A few moments later, they reached the rocks, and Ben helped her pull herself up on one so she could lean on it for support. During the swim, her breathing had become less frantic, but she had the look of someone who had fought a battle and lost. Exhaustion painted her features, and dark circles were already forming under her eyes.

"Are you doing okay?" he asked, as he pulled himself up next to her, finding a narrow ledge to wedge his body against where he could protect her from the brunt of the waves.

She nodded and grasped the rocks. "I thought I wasn't going to make it out," she said. "Thank you! You saved my life." Her voice was hoarse, but her eyes were bright. She coughed again, and more liquid sputtered out of her mouth.

"You scared me," he said, shaking some water out of his own eyes. He noticed some blood trickling out of her nose. "Your nose is bleeding. Does it hurt?"

She nodded. "A little. The air bag hit me pretty hard, and I think I got some cuts from that window glass, but I'll be alright. I didn't know I would panic like that under the water. I was terrified and couldn't seem to control myself." She reached out and gently cupped his cheek with her hand. "Thank you for putting up with me," she said softly, looking him straight in the eye. "How about you? Are you doing okay?"

"Now that I know you're okay, I'm doing a lot better." He covered her hand with his own and squeezed it gently. "And I'm extremely glad I've gone diving for lobster several times over the last few years. All of that time underwater really helped me stay calm and think through what I needed to do to get us out of that car."

She smiled. "Not to mention all of that ocean swimming you've done." She dropped her hand and grimaced as she moved her arm. "My shoulder hurts a bit from the seat belt, but that's not surprising since we just fell off of the bridge. I can't believe we survived."

Ben tenderly moved his hand to her shoulder and moved her shirt a bit so he could see the abraded red skin where the seat belt had held her in the car during the fall. She would have a good bruise there at some point. He watched her carefully, but her arm didn't seem dislocated or otherwise injured. The soreness she was experiencing was a small price to pay for surviving the fall into the water. The seat belts and the air bags had probably saved both of their lives. "You'll probably ache for a few days, but I think you'll be fine. You're moving it pretty well, and it doesn't seem to be broken." He glanced up above them, but from this angle, he couldn't see the top of the bridge or the railing. It seemed like they had fallen about forty feet into the water. He hoped their attacker had been arrested on the bridge, but he doubted anyone had stopped him after the car had gone over the side. The police really hadn't had time to get to the scene, and any of the onlookers who actually saw what happened would undoubtedly be scared of approaching him. The man had probably gotten away scot-free as the crowd of bystanders had grown and rushed to see what was happening with their car once it landed in the river.

In the grand scheme of things, though, it didn't matter whether the man had been arrested or not. What mattered was that Jordan and he had survived. They could hunt the killer down and arrest him later, once Ben knew for sure that Jordan was safe. And now, Ben also had an advantage. He had gotten a good look at the offender's features, and he knew exactly what the man looked like. He had also heard his voice. His first order of business, after making sure Jordan was out of harm's way, would be to start searching for the man who had sent them into the river and left them for dead.

He turned his attention back to Jordan. Why had he hesitated to renew their relationship? The enormity of what had just happened wasn't lost on him. She had been minutes from brain damage. If he hadn't gotten her out of the car when he had, she would have drowned for sure. He reached across the short distance that separated them and cupped her chin with his hand, making their eyes meet once again. "I'm really thankful that you're okay." The air felt thick and charged with electricity, and he couldn't seem to stop touching her. It was if by having that contact, he was convincing himself that she was still alive and hadn't been lost to the river. He wanted to lean closer, to feel her lips against his own, even though he absolutely knew this wasn't the right time or place to share a kiss. Her eyes were filled with questions, yet he thought he saw a yearning there that matched his own. Or at least he hoped he did. He pulled her closer and just held her, savoring the feel of her in his arms. She was alive. Holding her felt so right. Finally, he sighed and pulled back. Following his better judgment, he released her and turned his attention to their surroundings. First things first. He needed to get them both out of the water and verify that she hadn't sustained any serious injuries. Then he could think about the rush of feelings that was pouring over him and figure out what to do about it.

"Can you swim over there?" he asked, pointing to the closest shoreline. There were a couple of apartment complexes along the river, and one of them had a large dock with several boats moored along the planking.

"I'll do my best," she said, pushing some hair away from her eyes. "It's pretty far, but I'll try."

"You can do it," he said with an encouraging smile. He wasn't sure she actually could since she was still recovering from her near-drowning experience and had a hurt shoulder, but he didn't see any other options. He also knew that Jordan was tough and independent. When she said she would try, he knew she would give 100 percent, just like she did with every project or duty she ever took on. Jordan had always been strong-willed, and there were times in the past that they had locked horns for one reason or another and he'd ended up feeling totally useless. She was so self-determined, so capable. Yet, now he could see that personality trait with new appreciation. He valued her strength and fortitude. He also was starting to understand that just because she was so capable, it didn't mean she didn't need him, too. She excelled in many areas where he didn't, and the opposite was true, as well. Together, they made a formidable team. He shook his head, wondering why it had taken him so long to realize how precious she really was. It was as if a lightbulb had suddenly been turned on in his head.

He smiled, hoping to reassure her. "If you start having trouble, I'll help you." A new surge of protectiveness swept over him as he helped her back in the water and away from the rocks before the momentum could push her back and fling her against the stones. She started swimming the best she could, and he followed not far behind. He didn't want to get in her way, but he also wanted to stay close enough to help if she started struggling. His chest still felt unbearably tight. He didn't want to lose her. No, he couldn't lose her. Watching her come so close to death just now had made him see something with undeniable clarity. Gone were the lingering doubts and apprehension. Ben still loved her, and he wanted her in his life. He didn't know what the future held, but he did know he didn't want to experience any of it without Jordan by his side. Now he just had to convince her that staying together was the right thing to do.

Jordan swam slowly, unable to muster any more energy. She was exhausted. She knew they needed to get out of the water, but every stroke seemed to tire her further. Her arm was also hurting more than she wanted to admit, both from her healing gunshot wound and the damage she sustained from the crash and subsequent fall. Ben was right behind her, and she was humbled by the attention and care he had shown her. Not only had he saved her life—he had protected her and encouraged her when fear had enveloped her from head to toe. She said a silent prayer, thanking God for saving them from their fall from the bridge and subsequent drowning.

Suddenly she heard an engine in the distance, and she turned to see a twenty-foot center console boat heading in their direction. She breathed a sigh of relief. She doubted any of her enemies would have had time to reach them yet, so the boat had to be someone who had already been nearby and was coming to investigate the ruckus on the bridge. Hopefully, they were also coming to help. She saw Ben motioning to the driver, who waved in acknowledgment. He was a crusty older man in his sixties or more, with deeply tanned skin and heavy wrinkles from his years of working in the Florida sunshine. He was wearing tan shorts, a tank top and a baseball cap with a marlin on the front. Several fishing poles were lined against the back of the boat, and she imagined he had been out trying to catch a few yellow-mouth trout or croakers in the river only minutes before. She heard the motor slow, and the boat pulled up about twenty feet away from them. The driver stayed at the controls, but once the boat got closer, she also noticed another man moving near the fishing equipment. He was younger, maybe half the other man's age, but shared many of the same features. If Jordan had to guess, she would say they were related—probably father and son.

"Looks like you two could use some help," the younger man called loudly, making sure his voice carried over the sound of the boat and the waves slapping against the hull.

"Yes, we sure could," Ben answered.

The son nodded and threw out two life preservers.

Ben yelled his thanks and grabbed them both, then turned and swam one over to Jordan, covering the distance between them with a few short strokes. Jordan grabbed onto the white cord that surrounded the floating device and pulled it close, then put her arm through the middle. She breathed out a sigh of relief and said a quick prayer of thanks. She had been willing to try to swim to shore, but reality had shown her that she probably wouldn't have made it, at least not without a lot of help from Ben. This boat had arrived right in the nick of time.

The father turned off the engine and the son followed the life preservers by throwing them a floating rope. Ben caught it easily with one hand. Then he swam behind Jordan and put one arm around her, making sure to support her so her head wouldn't go underwater.

"Okay, we're ready," he called. As Ben swam from behind, the son pulled on the rope, guiding them to safety. Between their efforts, they slowly maneuvered Jordan and Ben toward the back of the boat. There was a boarding ladder attached to the stern, and Jordan was also thankful to see a small swim platform. As soon as she was close enough, she released the life preserver and grabbed the ladder, then carefully pulled herself up to the platform. It was slow going since her shoulder ached, but she could feel Ben behind her, ready to catch her if she had any problems. The son also reached forward to help, and soon she was sitting in the back of the boat on the seat cushion, water pouring from her and her clothing all over the floor of the vessel. The father immediately appeared beside her and handed her a clean folded towel.

"You doin' okay, missy?" His voice was gruff but caring.

Jordan took the towel and gave the man a smile. "Yes, sir. Thank you so much for pulling us out of the water." She unfolded the towel and wrapped it around her torso. "I don't think I was up for the swim to the dock over there. It's quite a distance."

"Glad we could help. We were nearby and saw your car go over the bridge. I'd say you're both in the blessed-to-be-alive category."

Jordan nodded. "I couldn't agree with you more."

She saw Ben hand up the two life preservers to the son, who threw them on the deck. Then Ben pulled himself up and into the boat. The father greeted him with a handshake and a clean blue towel as the son pulled the rope into the boat. At some point, Ben had ditched his suit jacket and tie, but it was still strange to see him coming out of the water in dress pants and a button-down shirt. Jordan felt a laugh bubble up inside of her. She couldn't help herself. "If I'd known we were going swimming today, I would have brought a bathing suit," she quipped.

All three of them laughed along with her. Today had turned out nothing like she'd expected, but they were alive. That was the important part. She had learned over the last few months to take hold of the joy she found whenever she discovered it. For this moment in time, they were together and safe. That was all that mattered.

THIRTEEN

Jordan wiggled her shoulder, adjusting her stance until the throbbing subsided. She was still a bit sore, even though it had been two entire days since her graceless fall into the St. Johns River. The doctor she had seen had told her that it would take a few days for the pain to subside, but she was impatient with the healing process. There was simply too much to do, and her hurt shoulder held her back.

She glanced over at Bailey, who was still typing furiously on her keyboard. Her polished blue nails flew against the keys, and once again, Jordan found herself admiring the woman's computer abilities. It wasn't just that she was freakishly good at typing at breakneck speeds. She knew how to find out practically anything by researching sources and accessing files that the creators had thought were all but invisible. She also knew how to navigate the dark net and how to find tidbits of information that just might help them close this case, if they could just point her in the right direction. She hoped that Bailey's current research would pan out into something useful.

Jordan was still sick about losing the notebook and the Mintax samples that they had gotten from Chad Peretti. On top of everything, she was also worried about Chad's safety, especially since he had refused Ben's offer of a protection detail. Hopefully Southeastern would leave him alone since he no longer had the notebook, but he was a loose end, so in her mind, he was still in danger until Southeastern was exposed.

She ran her fingers through her hair. Now they were truly back at square one. She couldn't help the frustration that swept over her as she watched Bailey work. At this point, Bailey and her computer skills were their only hope. Every other lead they had followed had crashed and burned. Even the hard drive they had found was still inaccessible. The encryption program was still giving Bailey fits, despite her impressive skills. Jordan had no doubt Bailey would eventually crack it, but it was a slow process, and in the meantime, they had precious little to follow up on to stop Southeastern's actions. To top it all off, Ben's boss was getting restless. Jordan knew the deputies had a stack of cases that needed their attention. They couldn't continue to focus their time on the Southeastern case if they didn't make significant progress, and soon. The sheriff wanted results, or he would shift his resources to cases where they could move forward. It was that simple.

Jordan glanced over at Ben, who was sitting back reading a file a few feet away at the end of the table in the Sheriff's Office conference room. She liked the way his brow furrowed when he was concentrating, and a whisper of attraction swept over her. He was dressed in his normal outfit of gray slacks, a dress shirt and tie, and his navy jacket was slung carefully on the back of the empty seat next to his. She liked the way he dressed for work, but he could be wearing anything, and he would still look amazing. He was truly the most handsome man she had ever seen.

She quickly tamped down those feelings and tried to focus on the more practical aspects of her ex-fiancé. He had some small cuts from the flying glass that were healing nicely, but beyond that, Ben had survived their ordeal unscathed. God had truly protected them from the brutal death their attacker had envisioned. For that, she was incredibly thankful.

She thought over Ben's behavior since their dive into the St. Johns River. He had been very attentive since the boat had pulled them out of the water and saved them the long swim to the shoreline. He had been careful to help her into the boat and had been by her side the entire time when they had gone to the hospital for checkups to make sure they had no hidden injuries from their exploit in the water. The doctor had kept Jordan under observation for a few hours since she'd needed rescue breathing to survive, but he had eventually pronounced her healthy and prescribed rest and reduced stress to help her recover. Then she and Ben had reported everything to the team, and they had discussed the case in detail, going over everything that had happened.

After the river, much of the awkwardness Jordan had been feeling around Ben had suddenly dissipated. It was as if he was finally at ease with her company, despite their troubled past. He seemed more relaxed and looked her in the eye more when they spoke. Even when they were away from the hotel, he was sticking close by, as if protecting her had become his number one priority. She had always known he was keeping an eye on her, but now his efforts were much more obvious. Jordan still didn't know if he had moved on to a new relationship or not, and even so, she had done her best not to assume that there was anything between them. She knew he cared about her as a friend, but she wasn't sure if he had any romantic feelings for her left. Either way, she was glad that he was becoming more comfortable in her presence, because when he was at ease, she was more at ease, yet she still didn't know if they had any future together or not. She had been praying about it and seeking God's guidance, but so far, she hadn't gotten any clear answers. For now, her solution was to keep her eye on the ball here and solve the Southeastern scandal. Then she would have time to analyze their relationship and decide how to proceed, if that was even a possibility.

"Eureka!" Bailey exclaimed as she pushed back from her keyboard and interrupted Jordan's woolgathering.

Jordan sat up taller, and she and Ben both gave her their full attention. Frank had also been walking by in the hallway, and at hearing Bailey's announcement, he had come in and crossed to her computer.

Bailey pointed. "One of my searches just came back with some very interesting information. It looks like Sam Delvers has invested heavily into Southeastern, and most of his own money is tied up in the company. If Southeastern loses everything, Delvers will, too. He has basically nothing left in his personal accounts and will be financially ruined if the company goes under. Even his house, or actually, his mansion, is mortgaged to the hilt and will go on the chopping block if Southeastern fails." She hit another key and the screen changed. "Two of Southeastern's main investors are in the same boat." She turned to Jordan. "Do you know Cindy Drake or Phil Johnson?"

Jordan shook her head. "I don't know Cindy Drake. I think Phil Johnson is a friend of the CEO's. I've seen him with Delvers on several occasions. Johnson was even at the labs a lot during the Mintax trials. I don't know much about him, though."

Bailey nodded. "Well, both of them will be financially ruined if Southeastern goes under. They'll have to start flipping hamburgers to make a living because they're gonna lose it all." She nodded sagely. "The pharmaceutical lab itself is also on the verge of bankruptcy. Their balance sheets tell a horrible story of mismanagement. The Mintax losses have basically crippled them. I bet their accounting department is going nuts right now, trying to figure out how to fix it. What I'm seeing is a lot of desperate people trying to pull a rabbit out of a hat to keep the company afloat."

Jordan's eyes rounded as Bailey continued.

"There's something else," Bailey noted as she brought up yet another screen and pointed toward the information she had uncovered. "Delvers, Drake and Johnson aren't the only investors that have put all of their eggs into the Southeastern basket. Southeastern has hundreds of investors, but I've found at least nine others who have also put almost everything they have into the company—and they are all attorneys that work at the same law firm right here in Jacksonville. Have you heard of the Baker and Davis Law Group?"

Jordan and Ben shared a look, but it was clear neither one was familiar with the law firm. They both shook their heads, and Jordan raised an eyebrow. "Should we know them?"

Bailey pressed on. "They're a large firm with about three hundred lawyers that do those annoying commercials on TV, you know, where they say they have an army of attorneys ready to help you win your case. I think they do mostly personal injury cases and class action suits. The nine attorneys that invested are all partners, including the managing partner."

"I don't know how often lawyers invest in pharmaceutical labs, but it seems strange to me that so many of them share such tight financial interests," Jordan intoned. "Why would a group of lawyers that work together invest everything they have into the same pharmaceutical company? Is that normal?"

"It does appear odd," Ben agreed. "And what does personal injury law have to do with pharmaceuticals? I thought those lawyers handled car accidents, slip-and-fall torts—those types of cases. Even the class action angle doesn't make sense. They wouldn't want to sue and cripple their own investment."

"Is there any reason one of these lawyers should know about the day-to-day operations in Southeastern?" Bailey asked.

Jordan shook her head. "None that I can think of."

Bailey sat back. "Well, it could be that one of these

lawyers is the one trying to hurt Jordan. These are some pretty powerful people." She paused. "Maybe we just need to keep searching for a connection."

Ben's brow furrowed. "If there is a connection, I'm sure not seeing it." The printer behind him powered up and a moment later, he pulled off a sheet with the names of the three Southeastern investors and the nine attorneys who had put all they had into Southeastern's coffers.

"What was the name of that attorney that represented Sam Delvers and cross-examined you when you testified?" Bailey asked.

Jordan looked up, thinking. "It was a woman with blond hair—really polished and beautiful. Hammond? Tammond? I can't remember her name."

Bailey clicked some keys on her computer. "Suzanne Tammington?"

Jordan snapped her fingers. "That's her. I might not have remembered her name, but I'll certainly never forget her face—or the attitude she threw at me when she cross-examined me. She's one tough cookie."

"You're right," Ben added. "I met her during a meeting with Delvers when they came to the office. She's a real piece of work."

Jordan raised her eyebrow but didn't comment. "Is she associated with that firm you mentioned—Baker and Davis?"

"She's a partner there and one of the nine primary investors, just like Delvers and the others. Everything she owns is basically invested in Southeastern." Bailey's lips flattened. "She certainly has an interest in whether or not that company succeeds."

"Sounds like it's time to take a trip over to that law firm and start asking questions," Jordan said enthusiastically. She stood. Finally, they had a new path to follow.

"Hang on," Ben said, putting up his hands, palms out. "Let's talk to Eddy. That's always got to be our first step when we have legal questions." He reached for the conference phone and called Eddy's number, using the conference function so everyone in the room could hear the call.

"State Attorney's Office. Donald Eddy speaking."

"Hey, Eddy, this is Ben Graham, and I've got Jordan, Bailey and Frankie here with me." He gave a quick summary of what Bailey had discovered.

"Tell me the name of the two other investors besides Delvers that weren't part of the law firm?" Eddy asked. They could hear him typing on his own keyboard.

"Cindy Drake and Phil Johnson," Bailey intoned.

"I'm looking for them on Martindale-Hubbell, the attorney database, but I'm not seeing either one. Maybe they're on Southeastern's board?" He typed some more. "Yes, they're both board members." He paused. "Can you give me the names of the nine attorneys that own a piece of Southeastern?" One by one he checked them but reported back that there wasn't much to find. "I don't see anything odd in any of these listings. I'm not seeing any other connection between them besides the fact that they all work at the same firm and made the same investments. There's no mention of the Southeastern connection, but that doesn't surprise me. There is no requirement that personal or business interests like that get listed, but I wonder about the conflict of interest for Ms. Tammington." They heard him hit some more keys. "Let me do some more checking on Westlaw about some of their cases to see if I find any patterns or problems that jump out at me from a legal standpoint. There might not be anything to find, but it's worth a look. I'll call you back if I find something. Bailey, if you can check into their backgrounds and search for connections between all of the investors, that will really help."

"You got it," Bailey responded.

They heard the phone click and Jordan reached over and pushed the disconnect button.

Bailey raised her eyebrows and turned to Ben. "How far, do you, ah, want me to dig? You see, there are legal ways to search, and other ways..."

Ben put up his hands. "Legal only," he said in unison with Frank. Jordan smiled at their quick response and Bailey's teasing laugh. She knew that in the past, Bailey had managed to steal over a million dollars through the internet and hide her tracks quite successfully so that even the sheriff's forensic accountants and computer techs hadn't been able to discover how she had done it. Bailey also knew more about the dark web and illegal computer tactics than anyone else they were aware of in all of law enforcement. Ben had told Jordan several stories about how Bailey had helped find a vital piece of information that helped solve a case while she had been working at the Sheriff's Office. She worked there as a condition of her probation. She was also an amazing asset because she had been both a defendant and on the side of law enforcement. That insight was invaluable.

Bailey had repented and returned the money she had stolen, and was leading a law-abiding life now that she was married to Frank. But Jordan didn't want any project she was a part of to tempt Bailey to return to her old ways. She could tell Bailey was teasing, though, and Jordan laughed along with her. There hadn't been a lot to laugh about lately. It felt good to have a smile on her face.

"Okay, okay," Bailey said with a nod. "There are a lot of social media platforms and other possibilities I can start checking." She winked at Frank again, then turned back to her computer and started typing.

Suddenly, Frank's cell phone rang and he spoke a couple of times, then hung up and stowed his phone again. "We've got him. We have an identity and an address for the man that pushed your car into the river."

"How?" Jordan asked.

"He got sloppy," Frank answered with a grin. "Not only did he let Ben see him before he pushed the car off the bridge, meaning Ben was able to give a great description of the guy, but he also left his fingerprints on the frame of the car. He probably figured you would both die in the river, and no one would check the car, but he was wrong on both counts."

Ben was instantly on his feet. "Let's go gear up. You can give me the details on the way."

Jordan stood as well. "Can I come, too?"

Frank looked over at Ben, clearly wanting him to answer that question. Ben was quick to shake his head.

"No, it's too dangerous, and you're safer here in the Sheriff's Office. After our dive into the river, I need to know you're okay so I can focus on the job I need to do."

"Besides," Bailey answered, "you can stay and help me with the computer work."

Ben gave Bailey a thankful smile, then turned to Jordan. He came up to her and put his hands on her shoulders. "I know Bailey's a pro, but I'm sure she'll find a way you can help her. The man we're hunting is a murderer. He's really dangerous, just like that man that chased you out of the grocery store. I really don't want you anywhere near the guy. This building is secure. You'll be safer here."

"Okay." She gave Ben a beseeching look. "Be careful, okay?"

"Deal," Ben answered. He gave her a smile, squeezed her arms affectionately, and quickly followed Frank out the door.

Jordan watched him go as the tightness swelled in her chest. What she hadn't wanted to happen was unfolding right in front of her—Ben was risking his life on her behalf. It was a bitter pill to swallow.

FOURTEEN

Jordan pulled out her computer and set it up next to Bailey's laptop, which was still connected to the Sparkses' hard drive. She doubted she could add much to the investigation since Bailey was such a technology expert, but it was worth a try. If nothing else, she wanted to keep herself distracted so she wouldn't worry about Ben when he was out in the field, in body armor, trying to arrest a trained killer.

"So, tell me more about the hard drive we got from Emma Sparks's house," she asked Bailey. "Are you any closer to breaking the encryption?"

Bailey shook her head. "No, still no soap. I've tried everything we talked about last time and then some, and I still haven't gotten in. I've got a code-breaking program running options, but it could take days before it gives us the key. So far, all I know is that the first letter of the key code is *c*, and there is a minimum of six numbers in the combination. I also know that there are a *j* and a *t* somewhere in there."

"Well, I've told you everything I could think of that I

remembered about Jeremy, but there is just such a huge number of possibilities, it's hard to narrow it down."

"Well, maybe we should try a different approach."

"Such as?" Jordan asked.

"Try searching for Jeremy Sparks on the internet and just read about him. See what you discover. The key code could be based on a childhood pet, or on something that reminds him about something significant that happened in his life. Those are things that wouldn't be readily apparent to his friends or coworkers who might not know his past."

Bailey shrugged. "It's worth a try, I guess. Now I really understand what it means to look for a needle in a haystack."

"And yet," Jordan smiled, "sometimes, people actually do find that needle."

They shared a laugh and then turned to their respective keyboards. Bailey's blue polished nails flew over the keys as she typed, and every few minutes, she stopped to take a sip from the cup of lemonade that was sitting near her computer.

Jordan could smell the fresh lemon, and she sighed in delight. Lemons and citrus in general always made her think of Florida, the Sunshine State, and her idyllic childhood growing up in West Palm Beach. Although better known for the oranges, Florida had their share of Meyer lemons, which were her favorite for making lemonade. Bailey had offered to share her drink, but Jordan could wait. For now, she was content to just enjoy the pleasant aroma of one of her favorite fruits and remember an idyllic time in her life when trauma and anxiety weren't as prevalent as they had been during the last nine months.

She opened up her browser and started searching. The name Jeremy Sparks was more popular than she had thought, but she got a more manageable number of hits when she narrowed the search to Jacksonville. She looked at the images first but didn't see any photos of her coworker in the boxes.

She ran the search again under *news* and came up with three articles. One was about a bank manager, one about a guy that worked at an auto-repair shop on the south side of town, and one story about how lightning had sparked a fire. She shook her head. Talk about random.

A thought hit her, and she typed a new search, this time including the names of both Emma and Jeremy Sparks. This search returned an arrest record for a woman named Emma and a listing in a people search site that wanted you to pay a hefty sum before letting you know if the person you were searching for was actually in the company's database. There was also a link to a story about a young man named Jeremy Sparks who had won several science awards at a small university in rural Florida.

Jordan pushed some hair behind her ear and checked the images under the same search. She scrolled down and smiled. There was a photo! It was of both Jeremy and Emma Sparks. They were much younger, but it was definitely her colleague and his wife in the picture. She wondered if they had been college sweethearts. She clicked on the photo and was taken to an old Jacksonville magazine that featured prominent Floridians who had made large contributions to the state in technology, business or science. She clicked on the article. There was Jeremy's smiling face again, and the article was talking about some work he had done on a competitive science project with Emma and a certain professor that had revolutionized the study of a certain strain of bacteria. As a result, the people of Florida had cleaner water.

"Did you know Emma Sparks was a scientist, too?" Jordan asked Bailey. "I'd never met her before Jeremy died, and I didn't know anything about her."

"No," Bailey replied. "I know we tried the usual password keys with her basic information, like birthdate, marriage date and stuff like that, but none of them led to the key code."

"Can we try a few new ideas?" Jordan asked.

"Sure." Bailey switched screens and entered a program that would try several variations of letters and numbers to see if they matched the key code requirements to open the hard drive. As Jordan fed her the information, Bailey typed it in and ran the program, which tried several renditions of the information by switching around the order and other common password techniques. None matched the requirements that Bailey had outlined. They found several six-number combinations, but no words that made sense and had a *c*, *j*, and *t*.

"I found the name of the bacteria they were working on but the letters don't match," Bailey said thoughtfully.

"Okay," Jordan responded. She continued scanning

for other options. "How about college roommates or friends from their college days?"

Bailey scanned another window where she had accessed Jeremy's social media platforms. "No matches. Any other ideas?"

"The name of their college and the graduation dates?"

That information was readily available in the same article, and Jordan fed it to Bailey one letter at a time since the name of the college actually met the letter requirements. "Nope, that's not it, either."

Jordan sat back, discouraged. She scrolled down on the article and found a picture that she recognized. It was of Jeremy, Emma and the same little girl that she'd seen a picture on the dresser in the master bedroom when they'd searched Emma's house. She leaned forward again, and quickly scanned the rest of the article. Who was that child?

"It doesn't say here, but I remembered when I searched Emma's house that I saw a picture of Jeremy and his wife holding a little girl. Here's a picture that's almost taken at the same time." She pointed toward the screen. "Can you help me find out who that is in the picture?"

Bailey shrugged. "Sure. Easy-peasy." She glanced at the article a couple of times, then started typing. "It looks like your friend Jeremy had a daughter. Her name was Charlotte."

Jordan was shocked. Jeremy had never mentioned a daughter or shown Jordan a photo of her. She wondered why the girl had never come up in conversation. They had talked about Samantha's son often enough—it wouldn't have been weird in the slightest to bring up other coworkers' children, but Jeremy had always kept the little girl a secret.

Her eyes met with Bailey's. *Charlotte* had a *c* and a *t*. Were they finally on the right track? "Jeremy never mentioned her," Jordan said excitedly. "Is she still around or did something happen to her?"

Bailey hit a few more keys. "Looks like she died from cancer at the age of three. She had leukemia. At least that's what her death certificate says."

"How awful." Jordan hadn't even known the girl, but she felt sadness for her friend and his wife and the pain they must have endured at the loss of their daughter, especially at such a young age. She opened up a note program on her desktop and wrote out the words *Charlotte Sparks*. Fifteen letters, and they still didn't have a *j*. They needed more. "What's the girl's middle name?"

Bailey typed some more, then looked up with a smile on her face. "Jade."

Jordan leaned back, matching Bailey's smile. "That makes nineteen letters." She leaned forward, the anticipation making her giddy. "What about her birthday?"

Bailey typed in the girl's full name and six numbers for the month, day and year of her birthday. *C-H-A-R-L-O-T-T-E-J-A-D-E-S-P-A-R-K-S-1-0-1-9-1-2*. The computer whirled and rearranged the letters into a different combination to make the key code, but they were in. The encryption was broken, and they could finally access the hard drive.

Jordan stood and whooped with joy, then reached over and gave Bailey a big hug. Now they were making real progress.

* * *

"So tell me about this perp," Ben asked Frank as he drove toward their destination.

"The suspect's name is Aaron Rich. He's a white male, thirty-five years old, five feet eleven inches tall, one hundred and eighty pounds. He was born and raised in Uganda by a couple of teachers from the United States who were there teaching at an international school for kids of diplomats. Apparently, he had a rough upbringing, and his father was killed when he was ten by a group of militants that were never prosecuted or even caught. He came to the United States for college, majored in—get this—accounting and had a few minor infractions with the law. They were mostly drug-related, but there was one assault and battery that was really nasty. He served four years in prison, then disappeared once he got out. Rumor has it he's a gun for hire. He was a suspect in a murder up in New Jersey, but he was never charged."

"Sounds like a real winner, Frankie," Ben intoned.

"Yeah," Frank agreed. "I was thinking of having him over for dinner on Saturday night. We'll grill up some steaks together."

Ben laughed at Frank's sarcastic tone. "Sure you will." His thoughts turned serious. "Sounds like Southeastern really knows how to pick them. This guy is a dangerous perp. We're going to have to keep our eyes open." He rubbed his chin thoughtfully, keeping the other hand on the wheel. "I wonder if there's any connection between Aaron Rich and the man who got hit by a car when he was trying to kill Jordan?"

Frank shrugged. "We never did identify that guy. All we know is that he was European. Interpol is still trying to figure out who he was. So far, we don't have a match for his fingerprints, or any hits from the facial recognition databases."

"Well, once we have Mr. Rich in custody, we'll have to show him a picture and ask him if he recognizes the guy. For all we know, they were buddies over in Uganda."

"Could be," Frank responded. He paused for a moment, then subtly changed the subject. "So, how are things between you and Jordan?"

Ben glanced over at his partner, but then put his eyes back on the road. "Complicated."

Frank raised an eyebrow. "Is that all you're going to tell me?"

Ben nodded. "For now. I'm still trying to figure things out." He let a beat pass, then another. "I still love her. You know?"

Frank smiled. "Tell me something I didn't know. It's written all over your face every time you're in the same room with her." He punched Ben good-naturedly in the shoulder. "Doesn't sound complicated to me."

Ben laughed in response, then returned his focus to his driving. They were close to their destination, and he looked at a street sign, then double-checked his GPS to make sure he was in the right location. They could see the house about two blocks away, but they pulled onto a side road and parked, wanting to approach the building on foot to gain the element of surprise. Because of the man's dangerous behavior and skills, the sheriff's team of four deputies had been joined by a SWAT team of five additional officers. The rest of the group was coming in different vehicles, and all team members were in radio contact. Once they confirmed everyone had arrived and were ready to move in, they began following their prearranged plan to approach the suspect.

The three-story Victorian house was in an older—but still very nice—neighborhood. It was situated on a large bluff overlooking the St. Johns River and looked like it had been built in the late 1800s. The home was one of several large estates that wealthy Northerners had built across from downtown Jacksonville back in a bygone era.

Aaron Rich obviously made a good living because the house was quite a masterpiece. It boasted an octagonal turret that rose three stories high and an ornate wraparound two-level veranda with hundreds of spindles. There were dozens of windows and a large regal-looking live oak tree that dominated the front yard. Ben guessed that the house was probably listed on the National Register of Historic Places.

Part of the group approached the house silently from the rear, making their way around the old but refurbished Olympic-sized swimming pool that was lined with lanterns, concrete benches and a slew of azalea bushes. Ben and Frank met up with two SWAT members and approached from the front, using hand signals to communicate. Ben and Frank quietly went up the porch steps and stopped at the front door, while the other two fanned out as the rest of the group surrounded the house. All of them had their weapons drawn and were on high alert. Frank gave a signal, and Ben reached over and knocked, standing away to the left instead of directly in front of the door.

The explosion surprised them, and the entire front door suddenly disintegrated right in front of their eyes. There was a flash from the explosion, and the loud blast sent them all reeling. Bits of wood, plaster and glass shot out and littered the front porch, and Ben and Frank were both hit with debris. A large hole now filled the space where the door had been.

FIFTEEN

If Ben had been standing in front of the door, he would have been instantly killed. Thankfully, the door frame and siding had protected him since he was positioned to the left of the door. Frank had been similarly safe on the other side of the door. The explosion did make Ben's ears ring and he was covered in fragments of rubble, but besides that, he was unharmed. He recovered quickly and signaled to Frank, who silently responded that he was also good to go.

Since Ben was the point man on this operation, he swiftly entered the house through the damaged doorway. The other team members quickly formed a single file line and snaked in behind him. Other SWAT members entered from the rear at the same time, and they all kept in contact with headset mics to alert each other about their progress. Ben's weapon was drawn, and he scanned the area, looking for the perpetrator, secure in the knowledge that his team had his back. As the point man, he knew he might have to make a snap decision that could ultimately be a matter of life and death. The assailant could rush them at any time, and he would probably be armed. There could also be booby traps or other surprises anywhere in the house like the bomb they'd discovered at the front door.

Once they were in the living room, each member of the team immediately moved to a combat position as they covered their area of responsibility. They had practiced this move on several occasions and had trained with a variety of scenarios. By dividing up the room, the law enforcement officers were able to ensure that they weren't in each other's way, and could also verify that the entire area was covered in case the perpetrator came at them.

"Sheriff's Office!" the team yelled, hoping to disorient or surprise the suspect, even though surprise probably wasn't possible at this point since the explosion at the door had obviously been meant for them. Rushing loudly into a room usually shocked the suspect for a few seconds, which was enough time to cover him with weapons and force the arrest. In this case, though, the assailant was nowhere in sight.

Ben motioned for two of the other officers to move toward the stairs. Most of the time, the law enforcement operations would run so cleanly that the entire arrest would happen without the law enforcement team firing a single shot. That's the outcome they hoped and trained for. Ben didn't have a good feeling about this one, however. The man they were chasing had a history of forcing confrontation and had obviously killed before. He probably had no qualms at all about taking out a few law enforcement officers if it meant he could escape.

"Clear," Ben called, and Frank followed him into the dining room that was to the left of the living room.

"Clear," Frank called, when they found the next room empty, as well.

They returned to the living room just as two team members were cautiously starting up the stairs. They had only taken a few steps when suddenly a round of bullets sprayed the staircase just above the officers' heads. They turned to engage, but Ben was quicker. From where he was standing below, Ben had the perfect angle where he could see the man standing behind the railing, using an armoire as a shield.

Ben aimed his weapon and fired twice, hitting the gun the man was using and sending it skittering across the floor. The officers on the stairs rushed up the remaining distance in seconds and quickly had the man within their sights.

"On the floor, now, hands out!" The perpetrator slowly raised his hands and then went to his knees. A moment later, he was facedown on the floor, spread eagle, and the two officers were frisking and cuffing him.

Ben's mind returned to the photo Frank had shown him of the perp right before they'd left their vehicle and started toward the house. He had no doubt the man being arrested was the same one who had both attacked him in his home and pushed their car off the bridge into the St. Johns River. He had a smirk on his face while he was being cuffed, as if being arrested was no big deal and he was confident he could beat the rap. The man's expression bothered Ben more than he wanted to admit.

This was the face of the man who had tried to kill not only him but the woman he had planned to marry. He knew he should be able to keep his feelings under control, but this time Ben just didn't trust himself. A thin sheen of perspiration appeared on his face as he felt the anger and desire for retaliation sweep over him. This was not how he was supposed to feel. This was a case just like any other case. His feelings for Jordan shouldn't play a part in it at all.

But they did.

He turned to Frank and gave him a pensive look as they secured their weapons. Thoughts of Jordan had been swarming around in his mind, and although he had pushed them aside during the operation, now that it was over, they had returned to the forefront of his mind in full force. "So, things are good between you and Bailey?" he asked in a low tone, but he already knew the answer. Whenever Bailey was near, a wide smile would cover his friend's face. That smile said it all.

"Oh, yeah." Frank said. "They couldn't be better. She's an amazing woman. I am truly blessed."

Ben couldn't be happier for his friend and coworker, but an unexpected twinge of jealously also swept over him. Frank's relationship with Bailey was solid. They both knew where they stood. With Jordan, Ben wasn't sure about much of anything, but he did know that his feelings of protectiveness and rage were overwhelming him at the thought of Jordan being anywhere near Aaron Rich. He stood, shaking off the unprofessional thoughts. He tried to detach himself. It was a losing battle.

"Make you a deal," Ben said to Frank as the other

members of the team escorted Rich from the building. "If you do the interrogation, I'll do the paperwork."

Frank raised an eyebrow. "You serious? I thought you wanted this one."

Ben shrugged. Doing the paperwork meant a lot more than just filling out his own report. He had been point on the situation anyway, so his load of the work was heavier than the others' to start with, but any large operation like this one would be reviewed and evaluated by the upper echelons of the Sheriff's Office. There would also be a team discussion of the positives and negatives that would result in another report that would be used to direct future trainings and correct any issues discovered. Usually, they all shared a bit of the work, so it was no surprise that Frank was surprised by Ben's offer.

"Yeah. That the guy took a shot at me and tried to take me out—not only in my own home but also in the St. Johns River." He shook his head, his hands fisted on his hips. "But what really gets to me is that he tried to hurt Jordan. I have to admit, I might lose my cool if I'm in the same room with him." He hated to confess his shortcomings, but there it was. Every instinct he had was to protect Jordan and defend her, regardless of the adversary he faced. He wanted to be the consummate professional in every circumstance, but this time, he just didn't think he could maintain his objectivity. He did not want to blow this case because he lost his temper in the middle of the interrogation.

Frank nodded. "I get it. I felt the same way when we had to rescue Bailey from Dr. Fredericks." Ben remembered when Fredericks had kidnapped Bailey and they had barely arrived in time to save her. They had come close to losing her that day, and Ben still remembered the relief and joy he had seen in his friend's eyes when they had rescued her from certain death at the last possible moment. He also remembered that he'd had to insist on driving to the scene because Frank had barely been able to keep his emotions under control when they had been rushing to her aid. The memories gave Ben some measure of solace, but he was still irritated with himself and his lack of control.

Frank gave Ben a nudge, drawing him out of his reverie. "Does this mean you and Jordan are getting back together?"

Ben drew his lips into a thin line as they started to leave and head back to their car. "I don't know. I did finally realize that I'm still in love with her. That's a big step for me. Jordan is still holding back, though. I'm not sure why. Every time I try to talk to her, she clams up and disappears. We haven't really had a chance to talk about where we go from here."

"Well she can't go too far since she's still in protective custody."

"True enough," Ben agreed. "I'll just have to keep trying."

"She's going through a lot right now," Frank said sagely. "Even if you have to close this Southeastern case before you have a real conversation, she's worth the wait."

Ben nodded in agreement. "Don't I know it. I just about went crazy when she almost drowned. You know,

I've been slow to trust her because I've been afraid that she will suddenly disappear on me again. I don't think I could survive the heartbreak of losing her a second time. But now it feels like someone has finally removed the blinders from my eyes. We can work on our trust issues, but I can't imagine life without her."

God was good. All the time. Ben knew he had a lot to be thankful for. His thoughts returned to the case as he watched the team lead Aaron Rich away. "Hopefully now, we'll get some answers."

Jordan typed a few more notes, then turned and frowned at Bailey. "I can't believe it. These numbers are even worse than what we feared. A full thirty-eight percent of the testing pool experienced seizures. Thirty-eight percent! That's horrific! And at the same time, only twenty-three percent actually had relief from migraines. It sounds to me like the cure is worse than the problem."

"Not only that," Bailey added as she skimmed more files from the hard drive. "Some of these other side effects are also terrifying. Look at these numbers—aren't those deaths that can be directly attributed to the drug?"

She pointed toward the screen, and Jordan looked closely at what she had highlighted, then leaned even closer to verify what she was actually seeing. "Yes. Good grief! With this information and the interviews the deputies already did when they were investigating, we can finally show how dangerous this drug really is. Jeremy is the one who signed off on most of these documents. I imagine that's why he saved copies of them all. They look like scanned originals." She chewed her bottom lip. "I also imagine that these are the only copies of these documents left in existence. I believe everything else has been wiped from Southeastern's computers and replaced with forgeries. None of these numbers match what they reported to the Food and Drug Administration."

Jordan watched as Bailey closed that file and opened another. They both skimmed the words together. "Their goal is to rebrand Mintax under a new name to sell in the US?" Bailey asked.

"That's crazy!" Jordan responded.

Bailey scrolled down. "Well, according to this, they've been working secretly on developing a copycat drug in China at a manufacturing plant that is hidden under so many layers of bureaucracy that it will be nearly impossible for it to be tied to Southeastern. The Chinese company only recently bought the rights to the formula for the drug. They claim in this article that they plan to make some minor alterations and then offer it for sale again. Apparently, the Food and Drug Administration is lax when it comes to enforcing the importation of unapproved drugs from certain countries like Canada, India, China and Mexico. If the pills are labeled for personal use, not heavily advertised and sold in quantities of less than a three-month supply, then the FDA probably won't stop them—especially since they wouldn't see a migraine medicine as a threat since headaches are common and not life-threatening." She paused as she continued to read. "Well, at least this way, Southeastern figures they can recoup some of the tremendous losses they had to accept when they developed Mintax, while also avoiding any liability if anything goes wrong."

Jordan took more notes. "They probably made some of the money back from the sale, but only a small percentage. I mean, the volume of sales coming in from a Chinese substitute won't come close to what they would have earned if it had gone on the market as an American-made drug. It's a workaround, yes, but that won't be enough to save Southeastern from bankruptcy."

Bailey closed the file and opened another. "That's weird," she said under her breath.

"What?"

Bailey hit some more keys. "I can't tell if Southeastern has already been paid for the sale or not. I don't see any large infusions of cash on their balance sheets, but maybe there's more that I can't see. These are only the public records. I guess it's always possible that they've hidden the sale to avoid taxes or other implications. I mean, they've wanted to avoid responsibility for Mintax since the beginning. Selling the formula and hiding the sale wouldn't be too much of a stretch, and it helps them avoid liability if and when the Chinese company gets sued." She closed one file and opened another.

"There's a really strange file here. It's in a totally different format than the other documents, and looks like it doesn't have anything to do with Mintax or Southeastern. It keeps referring to the Sunset Special train, and some man named Felix Jefferson."

Jordan turned back to her own computer. "Let me

see if I can find anything out about him while you're reading the rest of that."

"Sure thing," Bailey replied, her brow wrinkled. "Apparently, the train starts in New York City and goes all the way down to Miami."

Jordon typed in her search and quickly scanned the results. "According to this site, Felix Jefferson is an engineer on that train. It's called the Sunset Special, right?"

"Yes, that's right," Bailey confirmed. "But what does this have to do with Mintax? What do a pharmaceutical company and a train that goes up and down the east coast have in common?"

"Maybe nothing," Jordan answered. "Maybe that file was already on the hard drive for some other reason, and he just didn't erase it."

"That can't be right," Bailey noted, her tone thoughtful. "Look, the files were all added to the drive the month before Jeremy Sparks died. You can tell by the dates listed here," she moved her mouse to emphasize what she was seeing on her computer. "In fact, that file and this document were both added on the same date. This PDF in the file seems to be something about a train crash that occurred in Pennsylvania about three years ago. Do you remember that happening?"

Jordan shrugged. "Vaguely." She quickly skimmed the article. "Oh my gosh. It says that Continental Railways paid over $365 million to the victims of the train wreck. It looks like the engineer was impaired at the time of the crash." She raised an eyebrow. "Oh, Bailey, you don't think it's possible, do you?"

Bailey look at her with a question in her eyes, obviously not following her line of thinking. "What do you mean?"

"The law firm you mentioned earlier, you said they focused on class action suits and personal injury, right?"

"From what I remember. We can check their website to verify that if you want. Why?"

Jordan leaned back as the enormity of the situation hit her all at once. "Lawyers usually earn at least forty percent in fees when they represent victims, and if there are enough of them, a class action suit can be brought against the railroad. Even if all of the victims or their families don't choose to use the same law firm, they could still pull quite a class together and make a huge amount of money in one fell swoop through the crash and kickbacks." She threw her pen down on the table and felt nausea swirl in her stomach. "I think those investors are planning on recouping their losses and saving Southeastern at the same time. They're going to give Mintax to the engineer, and crash the Sunset Special."

SIXTEEN

Bailey's face looked horrified. It was the same expression Jordan was sure she was wearing as well.

"But that means hundreds of people could die," Bailey said angrily. She looked back at the article. "In Pennsylvania, almost three hundred people lost their lives."

Another thought hit Jordan as the enormity of the situation hit her. "This information was all collected before Jeremy died, which was over nine months ago. A lot can happen in nine months. Can you find out if the Mintax substitute is already for sale in the USA? For all we know, people are already using it." Panic and fear swirled together and formed a knot in her chest as Bailey typed her queries. It took her about ten minutes, but Bailey soon had an answer. Farnaprixolene was already available in small amounts by ordering directly from the Chinese manufacturer.

Jordan really did feel sick. "There's another class action suit waiting to happen. If enough people get sick, which they will based upon the studies we just read, Baker and Davis can make even more money by suing the Chinese company. They can claim the Chinese lab altered the formula in such a way that they are responsible for the deaths and seizures. Southeastern can avoid liability altogether."

Bailey looked surprised. "I don't know much about lawsuits. Can Americans sue and win an international case like that? It seems like it would be hard to hold a foreign company responsible."

Jordan shrugged. "I'm no lawyer, but I remember a while back there was a problem with a blood pressure drug coming out of India that was hurting people because it contained cancer-causing impurities. They were able to trace the problem back to the factory. We heard about it when I was working at the labs, and I remember discussing it during a lunch break one day with Jeremy and Samantha. We could check, but I'm pretty sure the victims won the lawsuit. I bet Eddy could find even more examples if we asked him to do a bit of research."

There were some noises near the front of the office suite, and Jordan looked up from the notes she was taking. When she saw it was Ben and his team returning, she stood and quickly approached him. He looked pleased and welcomed her with a smile.

"Well?"

Ben put his headset on the table. He was still wearing some of his tactical gear but had removed the helmet and assault webbing. He was dressed in all black, from his boots to the heavy bulletproof vest that covered his chest, and the clothing and gear made him look dangerous yet professional at the same time. He smelled faintly of gunpowder and the outdoors.

"We got him, Jordie. They'll be bringing him in for questioning in just a few minutes. I recognized him right off. He's definitely the man who broke into my house and pushed our car into the river."

"That's fantastic! I knew you would. I can't wait to hear what he has to say." She threw her arms around him and gave him a hug to celebrate, then realized what she'd done and quickly pulled back. It had felt fantastic to be in his arms, but she quickly chastised herself for reacting so exuberantly. "I'm sorry. I shouldn't have done that."

"I'm not sorry," Ben replied, catching her eye. His expression was suddenly serious. "Jordan, we need to talk."

"Yes, we do. Bailey and I just discovered..."

"Not about the case," Ben interrupted as he took a step forward and took both of her hands in his own. "Jordan, we need to talk about us. About our relationship. About the future."

Jordan took a step backwards, and he released her hands. "Did something happen during the arrest? Is everyone ok?" She was having trouble understanding why their relationship had just jumped to the top of his priority list when the Southeastern case was coming to a head.

"Everyone is fine. We'll be interviewing the suspect as soon as he is processed. We just..." Ben looked around the office, apparently noting the many people coming and going as they did their jobs. "We need some privacy so we can talk."

Jordan could see the hopeful glint in his eyes. Still,

she couldn't give him what he wanted, at least not now, when they were on the precipice of stopping Southeastern. She was bursting with the news of what they had discovered, but she could tell that Ben had other things on his mind that were taking precedence over everything else. "I'm not ready to do that, Ben. But I really need to tell you what we just found out."

"If not now, then when?" Ben pushed.

OK, so she was going to have to think about this now. She took another step back and pushed what they had discovered about the train and the new drug to the back of her mind. She had been ruminating on their relationship for quite a while but hadn't liked what she had concluded. Coming so close to death in the St. Johns River had forced Jordan to face some important truths.

She couldn't have done this on her own.

All her life, she had struggled for success and believed she had reached her goals on her own strength. She didn't like to depend on others. Even working in her lab, she had rarely delegated projects or tasks and had retained as much control as possible over the bulk of her assignments. Her problems with Southeastern were no exception. When issues started to arise, she had tried to face them and deal with them all on her own without help. Now she realized how incredibly selfish and full of hubris she had really been. She also realized how important God's contribution had been along the way. In fact, she finally acknowledged that she couldn't have reached any of her goals without God's help. Each day was a gift from Him. Maybe she didn't have to do everything herself. And maybe it was okay to depend upon others when she needed help. From now on, she decided to show others around her how much she valued their contributions, and she vowed to increase her efforts to collaborate and to show her gratefulness more to those around her.

She also was learning to appreciate the fact that Ben had gifts that were totally different from her own. She had always known that he had special talents, but she didn't think she had really respected all of his skills until now, when she'd had a chance to see him in action up close and personal while they had been working this case together. Ben wasn't a scholar and would never feel comfortable in a lab, yet his athletic ability and law enforcement skills were unparalleled. His unique abilities were undoubtedly the reasons she was alive today. She didn't think she had truly appreciated him or his skills until this Southeastern problem had risen its ugly head.

It was difficult to be thankful during adversity, yet her relationship with Ben was growing and changing as they spent time together fighting a common foe. She treasured the time they had spent together since her return and was so grateful that God had given them a second chance to grow in their relationship.

But even so, she truly didn't know where to go from here. Even though after today, she felt closer to him than she ever had, guilt still swamped over her every time she looked at him. She had hurt him so badly. By returning to Jacksonville, she had not only proven that she hadn't trusted him when she disappeared without a trace, but she had also pulled him right into the middle of this case with deadly consequences. Because of her, his life had continued to be in jeopardy ever since.

Even today, because of her, they'd had to arrest a dangerous mercenary. She knew arresting people was part of his job—and Ben had said that no one was hurt. But what about the next time? She had been living with the magnitude of the danger for a while now, but she hated the fact that Ben was now forced to live with the consequences of her actions. It wasn't fair to him. Ben was drawing closer. She'd thought he was going to kiss her when they had been resting on the rocks, but now, Jordan felt herself pulling back. She didn't want to ever hurt him again, and she doubted he could even forgive her for her actions in the first place.

She loved him. And because she loved him, she had to let him go.

"He's ready."

Both Jordan and Ben turned to face Franklin Kennedy, who had entered from a different doorway and motioned toward the interrogation room. "Do you want to listen in? I'm about to start the questioning."

Jordan breathed a sigh of relief. The interruption couldn't have come at a better time. She turned and moved away from Ben, trying not to react to the look of frustration on his face. "Definitely. But first you have to know what Bailey and I just found on the computer. We were able to break the encryption and get into the hard drive. It impact which questions you ask."

She waved Bailey over, and together, the two of them described what they had discovered, both from the hard drive and their subsequent research.

Ben shook his head, amazed. "To plan the deaths of hundreds, just to make a pile of money. It's inconceivable."

"Inconceivable to us, but apparently not to those men and women who are on the verge of losing everything. They are desperate people, and desperate people do a lot of stupid things." Jordan replied, although she couldn't quite keep the disgust out of her voice. "What we don't know is their timeline. We found the name of one of the train engineers for the Sunset Special, but we don't know for sure if they're planning to crash the train. That was just my assumption. It's possible they have another role for him that we haven't yet uncovered."

"Then we need to get this guy talking, no matter what. He could be the key to saving all of those people," Franklin said grimly. "I'm heading in. Why don't the rest of you watch from the observation room and let me know if I get off track and need to go in a different direction?"

"Count me in," Jordan responded, her voice filling with anticipation. She found herself oddly anxious to see the man who had tried to kill her and Ben, as long as she was safely in another room with armed law enforcement officers all around her. She didn't understand the man's motivation, or how someone could be so evil. But she hoped that somehow, they would be able to convince him to tell them what they needed to know before the Sunset Special was scheduled to take its final trip.

"Not me," Bailey said, putting up her hands. "I need to get back to the computer. Now that this perp has been put into the system, I want to see if I can find anything on him that we can use for leverage to get him to talk."

She turned and went back to her laptop, and Jordan headed to the observation room. Ben followed her into the small room with the two-way mirror separating them from the interrogation and closed the door behind him. She pushed some hair behind her ear and caught Ben watching her closely. His scrutiny always made her nervous. She knew he was incredibly good at reading her. At some point, she was going to have to tell him what she was feeling, but now didn't seem like the right time or place. She did know that she didn't want to keep hurting him. And he was right about one thing. They did need to talk soon so she could tell him that they couldn't be together. It wasn't fair to him to keep dragging him along. She glanced his way again and noticed he was studying her every move. She knew instinctively that he was still waiting for her to answer him.

"Tonight," she finally said. "We'll talk tonight, okay?"

He relented and relaxed his stance. "Deal. We'll talk tonight."

Ben flipped the switch so he and Jordan could hear the interrogation in the adjoining room. He was frustrated by Jordan's choice to delay in their conversation, but he acknowledged that they probably couldn't have talked right now anyway in such a crowded, public place. Still, he wondered at her hesitance. Ever since she had returned, she had kept a distance between them. He acknowledged that he had been doing the same thing to some degree, but now he knew what he wanted. Their dive into the river had made him see their relationship with crystal clarity. Jordan was the woman for him.

Still, for right now, all of their focus had to be on getting whatever information they could out of questioning Aaron Rich, so he pushed his personal agenda aside. The man had been processed in record speed so they could quickly interrogate him. He was a professional, so Ben didn't hold out much hope that he would talk, but sometimes people surprised him. And if he or Jordan wanted Franklin to go down a certain line of questioning with Rich, it was easy enough to pull Frank out, talk about it, and send him back in. He buried his concerns about Jordan and their relationship for now and put all of his attention on the job at hand.

"Can they hear us?" Jordan asked, pointing to the speaker.

Ben shook his head. "No. We can hear them, but they can't hear us."

Jordan nodded, indicating her understanding. "Didn't you want to be in there with Ben, too?" Jordan asked. "I've heard you talk about doing interrogations before. I thought that was something you actually enjoyed, and I know you're really good at it."

Ben shrugged. "I do enjoy it most of the time. Solving a crime is like putting a puzzle together. If I can pull out some new information from the perpetrator during the questioning, then I'm that much closer to finishing the puzzle. It's invigorating."

"But not today?" Her expression showed surprise.

"No, not today."

She raised an eyebrow. "I don't understand. That guy

could have real answers about Southeastern and their plans with the train. He might even be the one that killed Jeremy and Emma Sparks and Samantha. He could have a lot of the missing pieces to our puzzle."

Ben nodded. "Yes, he could. And I hope he does. I don't know if he'll talk or not, but this is the best lead we have right now."

"But you still don't want to be in there?" She took a step closer, a question in her eyes.

"Frankie is really good at interrogation, too, Jordan. He'll do a good job."

Jordan's lips flattened. "I know Frank is good, but I also know you're even better when it comes to interrogations. I've heard the two of you talking and joking about it. I really don't understand why you don't want to participate. I thought you wanted to help with this case."

"I do, Jordie." He fisted his hands. Didn't she believe him? Hadn't his actions over the last few days shown her how important solving this case was to him? He didn't really want to explain his shortcomings to her and his lack of control, but he could tell that his reticence was hurting her. How could he explain so she would understand, without making himself look unprofessional and weak in her eyes? He grimaced as he watched her pull away from him even further. He reached for her, but she moved slightly, just out of reach.

He let his hand drop but was considering his next move when motion caught his eye through the window. Rich was already sitting across the table, but Frank had entered, opened a file, and started reading over some of the documents. Ben decided he would wait to talk to Jordan tonight and get it all worked out. Hopefully, she wouldn't push too hard for answers between now and then.

He turned his attention back to the scene playing out in front of him. He studied the man who had very nearly succeeded in killing them. His hands were cuffed to a metal bar that was bolted on the table, and he sat unmoving, with a bored expression on his face. His eyes were dark and his skin held a dark tan, as if he spent a lot of time outdoors. His hair was a light brown and closely cropped in a military style. If Ben hadn't known him to be a killer, he would have thought he looked and carried himself just like many of the deputies that worked in the building.

Perhaps that was the point. Was he a law enforcement wannabe who hadn't been able to cut it? He didn't know the man's history, but everything about him was causing his blood to boil, and it was all Ben could do to restrain himself from rushing into the interrogation room and tearing the man limb from limb. This man had tried to kill Jordan. Ben never remembered feeling this much anger and hostility toward a suspect, and it was an uncomfortable, ugly sensation that made him feel frustrated and powerless at the same time. He had shared his shortcomings with Frank, but he really hoped he wouldn't have to go into detail with Jordan tonight. He was being unprofessional. He should be able to remain detached and do his job without emotion impacting his decisions and behavior. But he was finding it almost impossible to restrain himself from going into the interrogation room and wiping that arrogant smile off the man's face with his fists.

Franklin interrupted his thoughts by starting the interrogation. "I've already gone over your Miranda warnings, Rich, but I'll ask you again, do you want an attorney?"

"I don't need an attorney," Rich responded. "I have nothing to say to you."

Frank shrugged. "That's fine. You can just listen to me talk then. I want to start with when you broke into Deputy Graham's house and tried to kill him."

Rich stared at the wall, effectively ignoring Frank. "According to the official report, you broke the glass in his rear door window, then unlocked the dead bolts and made yourself at home. Sound about right?" Frank shifted. "Ben was able to knock the gun out of your hands, and then you ran away without it. It says here it was a Glock 19, nine-millimeter." He put the report down on the table. "Sweet choice. What did that set you back, about six hundred bucks?" Rich still didn't answer, so Frank pressed on, once again looking at the document. "This one was a generation five. Isn't that the one that lets you customize your frame size with backstraps that come in two different shapes?" He still got no response. "I think that one even lets you remove the finger grooves, so it is a lot more versatile."

Rich leaned back in his chair and studied the pattern in the ceiling, effectively ignoring him.

Frank was undaunted. "I can understand why you left that gun behind. I mean, it was the middle of the night, right? It was dark outside, dark inside. You had just lost a fight with a trained officer that left you feeling inadequate. You got scared, right? You probably didn't know where the gun had even landed, after Graham kicked it out of your hand."

Rich uncrossed his legs, then crossed them again.

Franklin pushed on. "Then at the river, what happened there? Did you get a bit cocky? A bit too sure of yourself?" He laughed. "I mean, the driving was incredible, I have to tell you that, but once you got that notebook, you took off your sunglasses, just to gloat. You had to know that Graham would recognize you, right? I guess you figured he would die from the fall, but you figured wrong. That was sloppy on your part. And then you left your fingerprints all over the outside of the car. Water doesn't wash those off, Rich. Even if the car does sink to the bottom of the river. Did you think we wouldn't check?"

Rich cocked his head to the side, but still said nothing.

"So you lived in a pretty nice house, Rich," Franklin continued. "I say 'lived,' past tense, because you're headed to prison and your days of living it up are over. But I have to admit, you had a pretty nice setup. Working for Southeastern must have paid well. So what's the going rate for taking out a scientist? Did they pay you the same rate for Sparks and Jordan Kendrick?" he paused. "Did they promise you a bonus for taking out the deputy sheriff who was guarding her?"

Jordan moved closer to the glass. "Why isn't he talking?" she said under her breath. Her voice was angry. "We know it was him. You identified him. We have enough evidence to prove his guilt."

"Sometimes they never talk," Ben responded. He

could see her frustration clearly written all over her face. Even her body language showed how tightly wound up she was inside as she began to pace in front of the two-way mirrored glass. He did his best to calm her down. "Others ask for a lawyer the second they sit down, and we have to stop talking to them before we get out the first question. Frank will keep trying. He's only just begun."

She rounded on him. "So why don't you go in there and get him to talk?"

"I can't force him to cooperate, Jordan."

She gave him an incredulous look. "You could convince him it was in his best interests."

Ben ran his hands through his hair. He *really* didn't want to explain to her why he hadn't gone into the interrogation room, but she wasn't giving up or giving him an out. He understood her frustration, but her behavior was making him even more unnerved. "Is that so? And how am I supposed to do that? There are no guarantees, no scientific formulas that will make him tell us what we want to know."

"You make it worth his while. Surely, we can offer him something to get him to talk."

Ben ran his hands through his hair and spoke before thinking. "Are you telling me how to do my job now?"

It was the wrong thing to say. He saw fire shoot from her eyes, and a muscle twitched in her jaw. She moved to leave the room, but he blocked her. "I'm sorry," he said quickly. "Jordie? Don't go. Please. This has been a rough day for me."

"If you didn't want to work on this case anymore,

all you had to do was say so," she whispered, her voice tight as she reached for the door. "It's obvious that this case is my problem and no longer yours. That's okay. I knew I was asking a lot when I came to you in the first place. I'm not mad. I'm just…disappointed."

"You sure sound mad," Ben responded. "And that's not it at all," he denied. Good grief, he was making a mess of things. A few minutes ago, he was trying to figure out how to tell her he loved her, and now he was in a deep hole and attempting to dig himself out of it. How could he fix this? Before he could even string another sentence together, they heard the door open behind them, and Donald Eddy strolled in, nearly bumping into Jordan as he did so.

"Hi, folks. Did I miss anything?" he asked. He had been totally unaware of the tension in the room but caught up fast. He glanced at Ben and raised an eyebrow. "Wow, I guess I did."

Jordan looked away, but Ben answered him. "Not a thing, Eddy. Rich hasn't said a word so far, except that he didn't want a lawyer."

"Right," Eddy replied, obviously not believing him.

The door opened in the interrogation room, and their attention was drawn back to the table where Bailey had joined Frank and was standing behind him.

"Find anything good?" Frank asked her, a smile on his face.

"Why, yes I did. Thank you for asking, Deputy." She turned her attention to the man handcuffed to the table. "Mr. Rich, part of my job is running background checks on suspects that get an interview, like you're having right now. Would you like to know what I found when I looked into your background?" Bailey looked at the man expectantly, but although he looked up and met her eye, he still didn't speak. She shrugged and moved a paper or two around in the file she was carrying. "I'll take that as a yes, please, ma'am. Thank you for asking." She raised an eyebrow. "Well, what I discovered is that as much as you like to pretend you're all alone in this world, the cold hard truth is that's actually not the case."

Rich's muscles tightened almost imperceptibly, but enough that Ben realized they had just hit a chord. He took a step closer to the speaker, his quarrel with Jordan momentarily put on hold. He didn't want to miss a single thing the man said, and if his guess was correct, the man was about to spill it all.

Frank gave his wife an amused look. "Hmm. Not alone. Is that so?"

"Yes, it is. It seems Mr. Rich here has a baby brother. And his brother hasn't been living large in a three-story mansion overlooking the beautiful St. Johns River. No, his baby brother has been in prison for the last three years, right here in the wonderful state of Florida. It seems he had some sticky fingers and tried to embezzle a large amount of funds from his employer. I say *tried* because he was caught almost immediately. It seems that Mr. Rich's brother isn't very good at crime." She paused and tapped the file against the table. "He's not so good at being a prisoner, either. He got beaten up pretty badly last week. Apparently, he doesn't work and play well with others."

A muscle twitched in Rich's jaw. Ben had to give it

to him. He was one cool customer. Suddenly, the suspect tossed his head back and looked down his nose at Frank, totally ignoring Bailey. "I want a deal."

Frank leaned back. "And why would we give you a deal? We've got proof that you attempted to kill a law enforcement officer and a civilian on that bridge. We've got witnesses and fingerprints. Our state attorney can convict you with one hand tied behind his back. All the rest is just icing on the cake."

Ben put his hands on his hips. Now things were getting interesting. He looked over at Jordan, who had also focused on the assassin's words.

"I can tell you more than just what I've done. I can also tell you who paid me to do it."

Frank raised an eyebrow. "And what's to stop us from researching that information and finding it out by ourselves? We've got our top people on that very assignment as we speak. Your entire financial records for the last few years will soon be sitting on my desk, and I won't have to give you a thing to be able to see them."

For the first time, Rich looked somewhat less than confident. His body slumped slightly in the chair, and he shifted uncomfortably.

"Of course," Frank continued, "if you could tell me something about their plans for the future, well now, that might actually be worth something."

Rich paused for a moment before saying, "I can give you what you want, but I need a really good deal."

"And what would this deal entail?" Frank asked. It was now his turn to pretend to be bored and disinterested. Ben knew that if Frank looked too eager, they wouldn't get much from the suspect in exchange for whatever concessions they made.

"I want to be sent to the same prison where my brother is serving his time, in the same wing. Even the same cell, if you can swing it."

Frank laughed. "Do I look like a travel agent?"

"That's the price of my cooperation."

"The same region is hard enough. Getting you at the same facility is nearly impossible."

Eddy smiled at Ben, then headed toward the door. "Looks like I'm on. You two have a good afternoon." He left and moments later, they saw him on the other side of the window in the interrogation room. He unbuttoned his jacket and took a seat across from the suspect as Bailey left the room and closed the door behind her. Frank stayed seated, unmoving.

"So you must be someone that can make a deal," Rich said in a matter-of-fact tone.

"That would be me," Eddy said caustically. "Donald Eddy, State Attorney's Office. State law says the courts can't force the Department of Corrections to place a prisoner in a specific facility." He tossed his pen on his legal pad. "What we can do, is ask the court to make a sentencing recommendation as part of a plea agreement. Nine times out of ten, DOC will place the defendant where the court asks, but there is no guarantee."

The suspect was quiet for a moment, and then he nodded. "That's the right answer, Mr. Eddy," Rich responded quietly. "I know the law, and I was just waiting to see if someone was going to come in here making promises that there was no way they could keep." He sighed, then looked Eddy directly in the eye. His body language made it clear he had made a decision. "I want your word that you will ask the court for a sentencing recommendation to place me in the same facility as my brother."

"You have it," Eddy agreed.

"And I want a guarantee that I won't get the death penalty. I don't care how long you put me in prison, but I need to be around to protect my brother."

"Deal." Eddy wrote out the terms on his legal pad and signed the bottom, then moved the pad so Rich could read it and sign it as well, even with his hands cuffed. Once it was signed by both men, Eddy tore off the sheet and handed it to Rich, then reclaimed his pad and pen.

Rich nodded. "I pushed their car off the bridge. I admit it."

"And who paid you to eliminate Jordan Kendrick?"

Ben and Jordan both took a step closer to the window, waiting impatiently for him to name the person who had tried to kill them both.

SEVENTEEN

"It's not just one person," Rich answered, leaning back in his chair. "There's a group of four of them. But the head of that group is Suzanne Tammington."

Eddy raised his left eyebrow. "The lawyer?"

"None other. She paid me $100,000 to take out Jordan Kendrick. Your deputy wasn't included in the contract. He just got in the way."

Jordan took a step back, unable to believe they had finally discovered who was behind the attempts on her life. But how could Tammington be the one? Tammington had been the one asking her questions when she was on the stand. She had been defending Sam Delvers and Southeastern from the federal lawsuits.

Jordan reeled with the information as Frank kept pushing. "Who are the other three?"

"Well, Sam Delvers, of course, and two other lawyers from Tammington's firm—Fran Sanchez and Martin Simms. I make it my practice to do a little investigating before I take on any job. All four of these people have invested heavily in Southeastern. They'll all be ruined financially if Jordan Kendrick gets the story out about Mintax. They can't risk someone revealing the history of the drug."

Eddy shrugged. "You're not telling me anything I don't already know. And there's more than four of them that are heavily invested in the pharmaceutical company. You're going to have to give me more."

Rich leaned forward. "That might be the case, but there are only four that planned all of this. I'm telling you the truth. I met with Tammington and the other three in person. These four are the brains behind the operation."

"How many times did you meet with them?"

"Twice with just Tammington, but three other times with all four of them." He looked away, for a moment, then returned his attention to Eddy. "Trying to take out the scientist wasn't the only job I ever did for them."

"Let me guess," Eddy said with a nod. "You did some traveling to China?"

Rich actually looked surprised at Eddy's question. "How'd you know about that?"

Eddy shrugged. "We know more than you think."

"Well, then you probably know that I didn't go to China, but my associate did. You know, the guy that got run over when he was chasing Kendrick."

"I know the man you mean, but we still don't know his name. Care to enlighten us?"

Rich chewed on the inside of his cheek. "John Hansen. He was an amateur. If I'd gotten that job first, we wouldn't be here talking today."

Jordan sucked in her breath at the man's comment.

He might just be boasting, but a part of her did wonder if she would still be alive if Aaron Rich had gotten the contract. The thought sent a chill down her spine.

Ben reached over and squeezed her hand, and this time, she allowed the contact. She glanced up at him, thankful for his understanding. It was difficult to hear people talking about her life and death so casually like they were discussing the weather.

"So what was Southeastern doing in China? And remember, I already know a great deal."

Rich laughed in derision. "So why do you need me to tell you?"

"To test the truth of what you're telling me," Eddy responded easily. "China?"

Rich shrugged. "They sold the formula for one of their drugs and are working with a lab and factory in China to make the new and improved version. Although you and I both know it's the same pill they tried to produce before and failed. They're already selling it through the internet and are looking at increasing advertising, production and distribution as we speak."

Jordan quickly turned to Ben. "But the drug causes seizures. It kills people. We have to stop them. They're already putting thousands of people in danger. We can't let this happen."

She hoped Ben would stick with the case long enough to stop Southeastern, now that they knew some of the company's plans, but she wasn't sure what Ben was going to do. He didn't get a chance to answer her before Eddy was pushing for more.

"Tell me about the train," Eddy prompted.

Again, Rich looked surprised, but he tried to act as if he didn't know what Eddy was talking about. He failed at his deception. His body language made it clear that he knew more than he wanted to say. "That's all I know," Rich hedged. "I helped set some of the wheels in motion in China. I can testify about what I know about that, and about the Kendrick contract."

Eddy leaned forward, apparently deciding to go in a different direction for now. "What about Jeremy and Emma Sparks? And Samantha Peretti? Did you kill them?"

Rich raised an eyebrow. "What if I say yes? Is that included in your deal?"

"Of course," Eddy said with a nod. "As long as everything you're telling me is the truth. I need you on the stand. You'll have to testify to everything you've told me here today and go into even more detail, but there won't be any separate charges for other bad acts we uncover along the way." He paused. "But if you lie to me, all bets are off."

"Then yes," Rich said, looking Eddy directly in the eye. "I killed Jeremy and Emma Sparks, and Samantha Peretti, too."

This time, Jordan reached out and squeezed Ben's hand. Finally, they knew the truth. A wave of relief swept over her, so strong that it made her falter. Ben was quick to reach over and support her in an embrace. Jordan was so overwhelmed with emotion that she allowed the contact once again, even though it went against her better judgment.

"So now let's talk about the train."

Eddy's question brought her right back into the here and now. She suddenly pulled away and turned to face the window once again.

"I don't know anything about any train," Rich insisted.

Eddy shook his head. "Remember how I just said you couldn't lie to me? I *know* you know about the train. I *know* you're the man that's supposed to make that happen. If you don't tell me about it in quite a bit of detail right now, our deal is gone. I can prove everything you've already said without any of your testimony. You have to give me more."

Jordan held her breath. That was a huge bluff on Eddy's part, but after a few moments, she could tell that it had worked. Rich motioned with his arms in a defeated gesture. "Fine. Tammington has an uncle that is an engineer on the Sunset Limited that runs up and down the East Coast. His wife is dying from some rare form of cancer, and he can't afford her meds because they're all deemed experimental by the insurance company. Tammington promised to take care of her aunt and all of her medical bills, if her uncle would take that medicine they produced in China while he was driving the train. Apparently, the stuff will give him a seizure because he has some sort of bad medical condition himself, and then the train will crash. Afterward, the law firm can step in and help with the lawsuits and make a few bucks."

Eddy was perfectly still, but when he spoke, his voice was lethal. "And when is this supposed to happen?"

Rich looked away and swallowed. Then he lifted his arms again and shrugged. "It was supposed to happen in a month or so, but because of the sheriff's investigation and all of the hassles you've been causing them, they've moved it up." He looked Eddy in the eye. "It's going to happen today."

Jordan took a step closer to the glass, trying to get an even better view of Rich. Was he lying? She was no expert, but he seemed to be telling the truth. "What do you think?" she asked Ben. "Is he lying?"

Ben shook his head as he considered the man's tone and body language. "Doesn't sound like it to me."

Frank must have agreed, because Eddy stayed in the room to hammer out the details of the conspiracy and the payment for the murders, but a moment later, Frank was standing beside them in the observation room. He was already on his phone and held up his hand, motioning that he was going to talk to them as soon as he finished the call.

Ben glanced at his watch. It was already past three in the afternoon. He waited impatiently for Frank to finish his call, wondering about the train's schedule. When did it pass through Jacksonville? Finally, Frank hung up and started to leave the room at the same time. "We have to go. That was the Continental Railways executive office. Apparently, Felix Jefferson is the engineer on the train today, but he has cut off all communication with the depot. They're trying to reach the conductor and will let me know when they get him, but in the meantime, we have to get to that train depot. The train hasn't reached Jacksonville yet, but is planning to stop here. The kicker is, we have to be there in twenty minutes if we want to stop him. It's only a five-minute stop, and Continental doesn't have anyone at the Jacksonville office that has any real authority to do something about that train."

Ben and Jordan followed him out and into the patrol car. Frank grabbed the keys and started the engine at the same time that Ben was contacting everyone in law enforcement that might have a chance to get to the train before them. It didn't look good. Jordan jumped in the backseat, and they were off, just as Ben reached the depot's security office. Unfortunately, they really weren't equipped to deal with the situation that Ben was describing, but they did offer to meet them at the depot entrance and escort them to the platform.

While he was driving, Frank's phone rang. He handed it to Ben to talk so he could focus on operating the vehicle. The lights and sirens were on, but traffic was sluggish and people were hesitant to move out of the way and let the patrol car through. It took a great deal of maneuvering to get through the streets.

"Ben Graham, Jacksonville Sheriff's Office."

"This is the Continental Railways home office. We haven't been able to get a hold of anyone working on that train. Either there's a failure in the communication system, or the engineer, Felix Jefferson, is blocking the line. In any case, we have three staff on board—the conductor, the assistant conductor and Mr. Jefferson. Look for them when you board in Jacksonville. Without knowing more, we have to assume the engineer is still in control of that train, but we have no way to talk to him."

"Got it. Thanks for the update." He hung up the

phone and turned to Frank. "Looks like it's up to us. The other train staff either can't or won't communicate with the home office, and Jefferson has cut himself off from the rest of the world."

"We have no way of knowing if he's taken the Mintax yet or not," Frank said with gritted teeth.

"Actually, we do," Jordan said from the backseat. "According to what I read this morning from the trials, once a person takes the medicine, the seizures start in about thirty minutes. The fact that Johnson has cut himself off but the train is operating normally means he's getting ready to act, but probably hasn't taken the pills yet. Let's pray he hasn't, anyway. If he did take them, then the timing suggests he wants to crash at the Jacksonville depot. If he didn't, then maybe he's planning to do it after the scheduled stop."

What she said made sense, but a sickening dread formed a hard ball in Ben's stomach. If the engineer was planning to wreck the train in Jacksonville, then they were heading straight into a situation that could well be fatal for all of them.

"Stop the car and let Jordan out," Ben said with a tone of authority.

Frank looked at him as if he were crazy, and Jordan protested loudly from the backseat.

"We might not make it as it is, Ben. I don't have time to stop."

A cold sweat suddenly covered Ben's skin, and he was tempted to grab the wheel and force the issue. He didn't want Jordan to die. How could he possibly protect her in such a horrible situation?

"I can't keep her safe, Frankie. We're trained for this. We always know death is a possibility. But she's a civilian. We have to let her out."

"I'm staying!" Jordan exclaimed forcefully.

Ben ignored her and clenched his hands. "Let her out, Frank. Please. I'm begging you." His friend was silent. He tried once more. "What if it were Bailey?"

Frank shook his head but kept his eyes on the road. "I can't, Ben. You know it, and I know it. Pulling over could be the difference between us catching that train or not. Every second counts. If we don't stop Jefferson at the depot, we probably won't have a way to stop him after he leaves. Hundreds of people could die. We can't sacrifice the many for one individual. You know that. We have to push on."

Jordan was touched by the plea she heard in Ben's voice, but she really did not want them to stop. If she died today, then so be it. In her mind, there had already been enough death caused by Southeastern, and she didn't want to be the cause of even one more life being lost because of their depravity. She reached over the seat and squeezed Ben's shoulder. "It's okay, Ben." She softened her voice so she wouldn't add to the stress that he was obviously already experiencing. "I know you want to keep me safe, and I'm thankful. I really am. But I couldn't live with myself if we missed the train because Frank stopped on account of me."

He took her hand and squeezed it hard. She could feel his desperate attempt to protect her from that touch alone. He didn't respond, so she tried again. "We're racing against the clock here. Please, let me do this."

He finally turned, and when he looked at her, she was overcome by the depth of love she saw reflecting back at her. "I need you to stay in the car. Don't fight me on this, please. At least do this one small thing I'm asking. I can't do my job if I have to worry about you and where you are."

The last thing Jordan wanted to do was sit in the car while they raced to stop Felix Jefferson from taking Mintax and crashing the train, but Ben had a very valid point. He was the expert here. This was his wheelhouse, and he needed to have the freedom to do his job without her interference. Part of her still wanted to argue. She was a competent, capable adult that could add, not detract, from the job before them. But she was finally learning that it was okay to let others take the lead. She was a scientist. She would let law enforcement do what law enforcement did best. "Okay, Ben. I promise I'll stay in the car. But will you do me a favor?"

He nodded.

"Keep your phone on, and call me if you need me. If you get to the engineer, you can describe his condition to me, and I might be able to help him."

If it were possible, he would have kissed her right then. She could see it in his eyes. Instead, he smiled at her with such tenderness that it made her heart melt. He mouthed, "Thank you," then turned back around to gain his bearings.

She loved this man. How was she ever going to let him go?

EIGHTEEN

"Sheriff's Office! Let us through!"

Ben and Frank raced along the train platform, heading toward the train that had momentarily stopped. The area was crowded, and they had to run around people who ignored their warning as they tried to get near enough to board. They had backup from the department on the way that was about fifteen minutes out, but they just didn't have time to wait for them to arrive. The four on duty security guards that patrolled the station had met them at the depot entrance, as promised, and had quickly led them to the platform. Now they were running behind Ben and Frank and trying to keep up. The deputies saw the train up ahead and finally were able to come alongside it on the platform. Just as they reached the last car, they heard the automated announcement that the doors were about to close. Ben jumped aboard the last car at the doorway near the front, while Frank managed to get aboard at the end of the car. The security guards were unable to keep up and were left behind on the platform. Seconds later, the doors closed, and the train started pulling away from the station.

Ben and Frank quickly made their way to the aisle that separated the rows of seats and started looking for the train's conductor and assistant conductor. They scanned each seat, looking for anywhere the two might be. They didn't come across anyone but passengers in the first two cars, but in the third, they found both bathrooms locked.

"Sheriff's Office," Ben called as he knocked on the door. Frank did the same on the opposite door, but neither one got a response.

Ben wiggled the door. It was locked tightly. "Anyone in there?" he called again, just to be sure and put his ear against the door. It was faint, but he thought he could just make out the sound of someone groaning. He took a step back, then kicked in the door. It opened and slammed against the wall behind it, giving a loud crash. The assistant conductor sat on the floor, curled into a ball. His hands and feet were secured with zip ties, and he was gagged with a red bandanna tied around his head. His hat was missing, but he still wore the rest of his navy uniform, which was now wrinkled and dusty. His shortly cropped black hair was graying at the temples, and his face looked haggard and tired. His eyes were open, but he moved sluggishly, as if he were drugged.

"I'm Ben Graham with the Jacksonville Sheriff's Office. Let me get you out of those." He pulled out his knife and sawed through the ties, then went to work on untying the bandanna. As soon as it was loose, the man worked his jaw to get the kinks out and tried to stand. His legs wouldn't support him, and Ben ended up half carrying him out of the bathroom and into the first seat near the front of the car that happened to be empty. He let him down gently.

"Thanks. The name is Grandy. Jim Grandy. I'm the assistant conductor of this train."

"How are you feeling?" Ben asked.

"Better now," the man said, still rubbing his jaw with his hand. "Felix gave us both some coffee, and the next thing I knew, I woke up in there, trussed up like a Thanksgiving turkey." He looked around anxiously. "Have you seen Joe or Felix? I don't know what happened to them."

"Is Joe the conductor?"

Grandy nodded. "We were all joking and getting along just fine. I wish I could remember what happened." He shook his head as if to clear the cobwebs from his memory. Suddenly, he sat up straighter and a look of alarm spread across his face. "Joe!"

"I'm okay," Joe answered. Ben turned to see Frank helping another man into the seat across from the assistant conductor. He was an older gentleman with a totally gray head of hair and kind blue eyes that seemed alert and intelligent, despite the fact that his body wasn't working correctly. "Has anyone found Felix yet? Is he okay, too?"

Ben shook his head. "Actually, we think Felix is behind this." Both trainmen looked surprised, but Ben quickly told them both all that they had learned, including the lack of communication with the home office.

Joe quickly felt his pockets. "Looks like my radio and phone are missing."

"Mine, too," the assistant conductor added. "Can we borrow your phone to call the home office?"

"Sure thing," Frank responded as he handed Grandy his phone.

"Thanks," Joe answered, nodding at Grandy to encourage him to make the call. "Let's get them involved as soon as possible and see if we can fix this fiasco. If the home office didn't even know there was a problem before you called, that's promising. You see, the engineer has to press this button within seven seconds of when the thing beeps every so often. Even if we lose communication, as long as Felix keeps pushing that button within the time frame, the home office will think everything is okay, even if they can't talk to him. If he doesn't push it, the brakes automatically go on and the signaler in charge of the train will give him a call to make sure he's okay. Felix has two phones, one internal to the train and a second external one that uses a mobile signal to receive calls and text messages. It even works in tunnels, but of course neither of them will work if Felix has shut them off."

"So since the train seems to be operating normally, that means Felix is still in control, right?" Frank asked.

"That's right," Joe answered. "At least for now. From what you're saying, though, that could change at any moment."

"So can the brakes stop the train?"

"They slow it down, but you need a driver in the cab to ensure the safety of the passengers."

Ben leaned forward. "So, worst-case scenario—if

we can't get in the cab and Felix is in the middle of a seizure, what can we do?"

"Well, something like that happened with a different company on a freight train. The engineer stopped responding, and it turns out he had a heart attack. The railway authorities had to bring another train alongside the running train to see if the driver was okay. Thankfully, there were other crew on the train who knew what to do, and the home office was able to talk them through it."

"Do you know what to do, if we find a worst-case scenario in that cab?"

Joe nodded gravely. "I do."

Grandy connected with someone at the home office with Frank's phone and asked for a supervisor.

Joe pushed himself up to a standing position. "While he's talking to the home office, the rest of us should head toward the motor unit at the front of the train. It sounds like we need to get into that cab as soon as possible to stop Felix from crashing this train. I sure don't want my southbound line to end up hurting anyone." He swayed a bit when he tried to take a step and glanced over sheepishly at Frank. "Can you help me, son? Looks like my legs aren't working too well."

"Sure thing," Frank said as he put the man's arm over his shoulder and helped him move into the aisle.

Ben motioned to the man on the phone. "Keep talking. The rest of us are headed to the cab." The three of them started making their way to the front of the train, leaving the assistant conductor talking to the home office and describing the problem. Ben grabbed the conductor's other arm, and between the two officers, they were able to move pretty quickly down the aisle.

Suddenly, the train lurched to the side, knocking them all off balance. "We'd better hurry," Joe said softly as they righted themselves. "That means the train is going too fast for this part of the track. Felix is probably no longer in control of the train."

The motor unit was two cars ahead of where they had found the drugged men, and the group rushed as quickly as possible toward the front of the train. Joe was able to press the numbers in the keypad by the door to enter the car, but once they got to the cab's door, they found that the second lock had been secured from the inside. No matter how many times Joe put in the code, the lock wouldn't release.

The train's momentum continued to increase, and they could all tell that the train was now racing way too quickly down the track. They had to get in that cab. Fast. They could tell they only had seconds before the train derailed.

"Felix has locked us out from the inside," Joe said grimly. "That was a safety feature they installed to make sure that if a terrorist took control of the rest of the train, they wouldn't be able to get to the engineer." The train lurched again as the train continued to speed down the track.

"So now what?" Ben asked.

"The good news is these locks aren't as heavy-duty as the ones they put on airplanes," Joe answered. "Those can withstand a grenade blast." He pointed toward Ben's sidearm. "I doubt these locks can stand up to a bullet or two."

"Stand back," Ben ordered.

The conductor nodded, and Frank helped him back up to the rear end of the car so they wouldn't be hit by a ricochet or piece of flying metal. With three quick shots all in succession, the lock came apart, and the door splintered around it. Ben pulled on the door and saw the engineer lying on the floor. Foaming spittle was dripping from his mouth, but beyond that, he looked unconscious.

Ben rushed to the man's side, and he heard Frank and Joe enter the cab behind him. Joe went quickly to the controls of the train and started pushing buttons, while Ben felt for a heartbeat. There was none. Felix Jefferson was dead.

A few seconds later, they felt the momentum of the train start to slow, and eventually, the train stopped completely.

Joe mopped the sweat from his forehead with his sleeve and leaned back in the engineer's chair, a look of grim satisfaction on his face. "We did it, boys. We stopped the train." He looked sadly down at Felix. "Is he dead?"

Ben nodded. "I'm afraid so. Looks like you were right, though. We got here just in time to stop the crash and save the passengers. It's a shame we couldn't save Felix, too."

Despite the engineer's death, Ben suddenly felt as though a huge burden had been lifted from his shoulders. Relief swamped over him, and he said a silent prayer of thankfulness. He knew they couldn't have done this without God's help. He looked over at Frank. "What do you think about going with me to arrest some lawyers?"

Frank smiled. "I think that's an excellent idea."

NINETEEN

Jordan walked over to the seating area of the general aviation section of the small airport and opened the magazine she had been carrying. She tried to look as nonchalant as possible as she flipped carelessly through the pages. Suzanne Tammington looked up from her seat about three feet away. She glanced at the new arrival, then did a double take. A worried look crossed her face. "What are you doing here?"

"I'm here to see you off. After all you've put me through and all the harm you've caused, I think it's only fitting that I get to see you up close and personal as your world comes crashing down around you."

Suzanne glanced around cautiously but didn't see anything out of the ordinary. There didn't appear to be anybody else nearby except for the gate agent, who seemed absorbed in his work at a kiosk near the front of the room. The lack of visible threats made the attorney's confidence soar.

"I don't know what you're talking about," she said haughtily. "In a few short hours, I'll be sitting on the beach, sipping a drink and watching the dolphins playing in the surf."

Jordan raised an eyebrow. "You won't get away with it."

"I still don't know what you're talking about," she repeated. "I've done nothing to you beyond rip you apart on the witness stand." She looked down her nose at Jordan, and there was a sly smirk on her face. "It's not my fault you buckled under pressure."

"Hiring someone to kill me certainly sounds like something. Was I really that big of threat to you and Southeastern?"

The attorney busied herself by putting a file she had been reading back in her burgundy leather briefcase. Finally, she turned back and looked Jordan directly in the eye. "You are nothing to me. I made mincemeat of you on the stand during the trial, and I'll beat any charge you send my way. You see, Ms. Kendrick, I always get what I want. If I want you to say something on the stand, I'll get it from you. If I want you to leave South Carolina and go running for home, I'll make it happen." She leaned closer. "If I want you dead, then you'll end up dead. It's that simple."

Jordan ignored the look of hatred emanating from the woman's eyes, despite the chill it sent down her spine. "Yet, here I am. I didn't drown in that river, and your mercenaries haven't been able to kill me yet. You failed, Miss Tammington." She leaned forward herself. "And there's something I've been wanting to tell you."

"Oh, really?" The attorney laughed. "And what is that?"

Jordan smiled. "You're under arrest."

The room was suddenly filled with law enforcement officers, all with their weapons pointed toward the attorney.

"On the floor, now!" Ben yelled, coming up closest to the woman. "Get on your knees!"

The attorney glared at Jordan, then slowly sank down on the floor with her hands up. She was smart enough to know that there was no escaping the inevitable.

Tammington shot Jordan another look of hatred, but Jordan was too elated to care. She smiled at Ben and pulled the wire out from beneath her shirt. "Did you get what you needed?" she asked.

"Oh, yes," Ben said with a returning smile as he watched Frank put the woman in handcuffs and pull her to her feet. "It seems Ms. Tammington here will be going to prison for quite a long time. Do you think she'll look good in orange?"

"Hmm," Jordan said, as she tapped her cheek with her finger. "That's a good question. I guess we'll just have to see once she gets that pretty jumpsuit. I don't think they come in designer colors."

Frank shook his head at the two of them and laughed, then leaned toward the attorney. "You have the right to remain silent. If you give up the right to remain silent, anything you say can and will be used against you…."

"I know my rights!" Tammington snapped.

"Yes," Ben nodded. "I'm sure you do."

They led her out the door and toward the waiting patrol car. Tammington had been the last of the attorneys to get arrested. The other two attorneys had been detained at the firm's offices, and Sam Delvers had been taken into custody in his own home. Of the four, only Suzanne Tammington had tried to escape. She alone had been in contact with Felix Jefferson on the train and had been the first to know that the crash had been stopped by law enforcement. A call to Tammington had been the last one recorded on Felix's phone—presumably to let her know that he had taken the Mintax. As soon as she realized that their plans had failed, she had immediately headed to the small commercial airport, used mostly by wealthy individuals who had access to private jets.

Ben drew Jordan into his arms, unmindful of the other law enforcement agents that were securing the scene. "It's over, Jordan. You're safe, and everyone that tried to hurt you has been arrested."

"You have been amazing," she murmured against his shirt. "You'll never know how thankful I am." She pulled back so he could see the truth mirrored in her eyes. "I really couldn't have done this without you."

"Yes, you could have. I know you, Jordan. You would have found a way," he responded.

She shook her head. "I know sometimes I think I can do everything myself, but if there's one thing I've learned through all of this, it's that it's okay to ask for help when I need it. And I needed it. I really did. You saved my life. More than once."

A wave of sadness swept over her. Now that the case was over, it was time for her to move on. The thought bothered her more than she wanted to admit. Still, she had to stick to her resolve. She still loved him, which meant she still had to let him go. The danger had passed, but she needed to disappear again and let Ben get back to his life. She had already disrupted him enough. "I guess I'll get packed up at the hotel and be on my way."

Ben grasped both of her hands, then looked around them. Several officers worked nearby, all pretending not to be watching or listening in to Ben and Jordan's conversation. He knew they meant well, but this was one conversation he wanted to have in private. He led her to a corner of the room where they wouldn't be overheard.

"Jordan, I really don't want you to go."

She squeezed his hands, then released him. "That's sweet of you to say. But you didn't even want to help out with the interrogation, so I know I've overstayed my welcome and pushed you hard to do something you really didn't want to do. I'm sorry about that, by the way. I didn't want to put you in danger in the first place."

"Look, Jordie, we still haven't had a chance to talk. So much has been happening, and with this case coming to a head, well..." He kicked at the floor as he shifted. He didn't want to admit this, but if he didn't, she might not believe the rest of what he was going to tell her. And he desperately wanted her to believe it. "I need to explain what happened when Aaron Rich was arrested." She looked up at him, and her eyes were luminous. She was giving him her full attention, and there was so much trust and caring he saw there that he knew a moment of dread. Would she hate him for being so out of control? So unprofessional? Either way, he had to be honest with her. "When I'm working as a law enforcement officer, I try really hard to stay objective. I follow the law. I do what needs to be done to the best of my ability. But with Aaron Rich, I couldn't do that. After he was arrested, it was all I could do not to attack the man. I didn't care that he had come after me. We have people trying to take us down all the time. I never take that personally. But when that man came after you, the woman that I love, I just couldn't handle it."

He looked away, and there were tears in his eyes. He was laying himself bare in front of her, right there in the airport lobby. He took a moment to compose himself, then he looked her in the eye again. She had the grace not to interrupt him and to let him finish telling her what he so obviously needed to say. "I wanted to hurt him, to physically hurt him, and I knew then that I was too close to this case. I had to take a step back and let Frank handle it. If I hadn't, I would have messed it up, and we wouldn't have been able to use any of his testimony, because I would have lost my temper." He looked away again. "I couldn't have gotten him to talk, as much as I wanted to, because I would have ended up doing something stupid, which would have messed up the legal case. I didn't want to tell you about my shortcomings because you're always so capable. I didn't want you to think less of me."

Jordan reached up and cupped his chin with her hand, then turned his face to hers again. "I could never think less of you. You're my hero. I appreciate you explaining what you were thinking. But don't you see that what you just told me makes me love you even more?"

His brow furrowed. Her reaction was not what he

had expected. He anticipated disappointment—maybe even disgust. Yet, he saw the truth of her love in her eyes. "You love me?"

She smiled. "Of course I do. You're the man of my dreams. It's only when I'm with you that everything is right in my life. When I was away in South Carolina, I was so lost. When I'm with you, I can be the best version of myself."

"But you've been distant, pulling yourself away whenever I tried to get close. I don't understand."

"Oh, Ben." It was her turn to look away. She bit her bottom lip, and he saw her body start to shake. She took a moment and then faced him again. "I should have trusted you from the start, but I didn't, and I ended up hurting you. I never wanted to do that. This whole time, I've been afraid that since I shattered your trust, you didn't want me anymore. I thought you were only helping me because you felt sorry for me. Can you ever forgive me?"

He pulled her into his arms. "We should have talked a long time ago. Sure, I was hurt that you left like you did, but I've forgiven you, and I understand why you did it. You were trying to protect me. I get that."

"Yes, I was trying to protect you. That was the biggest reason why I went into witness protection. But if I'm being completely honest, I have to tell you that a part of me also wanted to solve my problems all on my own." She squeezed him and rested her head on his chest. "I've learned that it's okay to get help now and then. I'm sorry it took me so long to figure that out."

He rubbed her back gently, enjoying the closeness.

"Well, the good part is, our relationship now seems stronger than ever." He turned her face up to his. "Promise me you won't leave again. Please? I want you to stay. Please stay and be my wife."

"Are you sure?"

"Absolutely." He leaned down and gently covered her lips with his own. It was a kiss full of love and promise. Finally, he pulled back and caressed her cheek with his hand. "God is the God of second chances. I see that now. He's given us a second chance, and I want to grab a hold with both hands and never let go. Please say you'll stay and be my wife."

"I'll stay." Jordan smiled as she grasped his hand and squeezed it. "You're the love of my life. I'd be honored to marry you."

EPILOGUE

"You're not supposed to see my dress before the wedding!" Jordan protested, as Ben strolled into the hotel room and swung her around in a circle. He was wearing his tux and looked simply magnificent. The suit accented his broad shoulders, and the happiness in his face made him look more handsome than she'd ever seen him before. She laughed in delight and fell against him as the dizziness hit. "Now you have to pretend to be surprised when I walk down the aisle."

He laughed, his brown eyes twinkling. Frank walked up behind him, also in a tux but carrying a small red rosebud and a long stickpin. "I told this guy to wait, but does he listen to me, his best man? Nope, not at all. He never learns." He took the flower and pinned it to Ben's lapel as the two separated. "There you go. Now that you're properly dressed, you can rush off and see your fiancée and tell her the news."

Jordan laughed. She knew Frank was a fastidious dresser and took great care in his appearance. He could rarely be seen without a jacket and tie, unless he was headed to play softball on the sheriff's team or to see his alma mater, Florida State University, competing in a sporting event. As usual, his suit was immaculate, and he had the look of a man who had gone to great pains to make sure his appearance was crisp and formal. He was apparently trying to make sure Ben was also at the top of his game as well, but something had distracted Ben and brought him to her door. Jordan was amused at her fiancé's exuberance.

"We just discovered some news about the case, and I didn't want to wait to tell you," Ben said as he played with a curl that hung by her face. He wrapped her hair around his finger, then leaned in and gave her a kiss before releasing it. "Sam Delvers, the CEO of Southeastern, just confessed that he has ties to the marshal's office. Remember how we couldn't figure out why they did such a poor job of protecting you? Usually the marshals are a top-notch group. Well the marshal assigned to your case is Delvers's second cousin. They grew up together, and even used to stay at each other's houses during the summers when they were in high school."

Jordan shook her head. "That explains so much!" she said emphatically. "Of course, the marshal wasn't concerned when I reported that man following me, or when he tried to kill me. Tammington and Delvers probably organized the hit and sent the mercenary up there, then told the marshal to look the other way. The marshal probably even gave him my address at the safe house."

"Well, the marshal was just arrested and charged, so you no longer have to worry about him." He smiled. "And, another connection was just revealed. Tammington also had ties to the prosecuting attorney. Apparently, Tammington had represented his parents in a big case down in Miami. Eddy discovered the conflict and reported it. Before the case, both attorneys should have reported the conflict themselves, but neither one did. Apparently, the investigators have even uncovered proof that the two colluded to throw the case. You never really had a chance to stop Southeastern in court. Not a fair chance, anyway." He paused. "The prosecutor just lost his job, and is getting disbarred. He won't be stepping anywhere near a courtroom for the rest of his career."

Ben kissed her again. "I guess I could have waited to tell you all of this, but I wanted you to know so we could put it all behind us before you walked down the aisle. I know you were wondering about the marshal and all, so now we have answers."

Jordan smiled and bit her bottom lip. "I'm glad you did. I have to admit, it puts my mind at ease. And today, I want all of my focus to be where it should be—on my handsome groom!" She ran her fingers over his lips and reveled at the softness. Could this big wonderful man really be about to become her husband? God had truly blessed her beyond measure. "I love you, Benjamin Graham. I want to be with you forever. God has given us this second chance, and I'm not going to waste it."

Ben smiled, his eyes dancing. "I love you, too, Jordan. No matter what the future brings, I can face it head-on, as long as I have you by my side."

* * * * *

Don't miss Kathleen Tailer's
next thrilling novel,
available September 2020 wherever
Love Inspired Suspense books
and ebooks are sold.

WE HOPE YOU ENJOYED
THIS BOOK FROM

LOVE INSPIRED SUSPENSE
INSPIRATIONAL ROMANCE

Courage. Danger. Faith.

Find strength and determination in stories
of faith and love in the face of danger.

6 NEW BOOKS AVAILABLE EVERY MONTH!

LISHALO2020

COMING NEXT MONTH FROM
Love Inspired Suspense

Available May 5, 2020

CHASING SECRETS
True Blue K-9 Unit: Brooklyn • by Heather Woodhaven

When Karenna Pressley stumbles on a man trying to drown her best friend, he turns his sights on her—and she barely escapes. Now Karenna's the only person who can identify the attacker, but can her ex-boyfriend, Officer Raymond Morrow, and his K-9 partner keep her alive?

WITNESS PROTECTION UNRAVELLED
Protected Identities • by Maggie K. Black

Living in witness protection won't stop Travis Stone from protecting two orphaned children whose grandmother was just attacked. But when his former partner, Detective Jessica Eddington, arrives to convince him to help bring down the group that sent him into hiding, agreeing to the mission could put them all at risk.

UNDERCOVER THREAT
by Sharon Dunn

Forced to jump ship when her cover's blown, DEA agent Grace Young's rescued from criminals and raging waters by her ex-husband, Coast Guard swimmer Dakota Young. Now they must go back undercover as a married couple to take down the drug ring, but can they live to finish the assignment?

ALASKAN MOUNTAIN MURDER
by Sarah Varland

After her aunt disappears on a mountain trail, single mom Cassie Hawkins returns to Alaska...and becomes a target. With both her life and her child's on the line, Cassie needs help. And relying on Jake Stone—her son's secret father—is the only way they'll survive.

HOSTAGE RESCUE
by Lisa Harris

A hike turns deadly when two armed men take Gwen Ryland's brother hostage and shove her from a cliff. Now with Caden O'Callaghan, a former army ranger from her past, by her side, Gwen needs to figure out what the men want in time to save her brother...and herself.

UNTRACEABLE EVIDENCE
by Sharee Stover

It's undercover ATF agent Randee Jareau's job to make sure the government's 3-D printed "ghost gun" doesn't fall into the wrong hands. So when someone goes after scientist Ace Steele, she must protect him...before she loses the undetectable weapon *and* its creator.

LOOK FOR THESE AND OTHER LOVE INSPIRED BOOKS WHEREVER BOOKS ARE SOLD, INCLUDING MOST BOOKSTORES, SUPERMARKETS, DISCOUNT STORES AND DRUGSTORES.

LISCNM0420

SPECIAL EXCERPT FROM

Return to River Haven, where a mysterious stranger will bring two lonely hearts together...

When Amish quilt shop owner Joanna Kohler finds an injured woman on her property, she is grateful for the help of fellow store owner Noah Troyer, who feels it's his duty to aid, especially when danger draws close.

Read on for a sneak peek at
Amish Protector *by Marta Perry*

Home again. Joanna Kohler moved to the door as the small bus that connected the isolated Pennsylvania valley towns drew up to the stop at River Haven.

Another few steps brought her to the quilt shop, where she paused, gazing with pleasure at the window display she'd put up over the weekend. Smiling at her own enthusiasm for the shop she and her aunt ran, she rounded the corner and headed down the alley toward the enclosed stairway that led to their apartment above the shop.

The glow of lamplight from the back of the hardware store next door allowed her to cross to the yard to her door without her flashlight. Noah Troyer, her neighbor, must be working late. Her side of the building was in darkness, since Aunt Jessie was away.

Joanna fitted her key into the lock, and the door swung open almost before she'd turned it. Collecting her packages, she started up the steps, not bothering to switch on her penlight. The stairway was familiar enough, and she didn't need—

Her foot hit something. Joanna stumbled forward, grabbing at the railing to keep herself from falling. What in the world...? Reaching out, her hand touched something soft, warm, something that felt like human flesh. She gasped, pulling back.

Clutching her self-control with all her might, Joanna grasped her penlight, aimed it and switched it on.

A woman lay sprawled on the stairs. The beam touched high-heeled boots, jeans, a suede jacket. Stiffening her courage, Joanna aimed the light higher. The woman was young, *Englisch*, with brown hair that hung to her shoulders. It might have been soft and shining if not for the bright blood that matted it.

Panic sent her pulses racing, and she uttered a silent prayer, reaching tentatively to touch the face. Warm...thank the *gut* Lord. She...whoever she was...was breathing. Now Joanna must get her the help she needed.

Hurrying, fighting for control, Joanna scrambled back down the steps. She burst out into the quiet yard. Even as she stepped outside, she realized it would be faster to go to Noah's back door than around the building.

Running now, she reached the door in less than a minute and pounded on it, calling his name. "Noah!"

PHMPEXP0420

After a moment that felt like an hour, light spilled out. Noah Troyer filled the doorway, staring at her, his usually stoic face startled. “Joanna, what’s wrong? Are you hurt?”

A shudder went through her. “Not me, no. There’s a woman…” She pointed toward her door, explanations deserting her. *“Komm, schnell.”* Grabbing his arm, she tugged him along.

By the time they reached her door, Noah was ahead of her. “We’ll need a light.”

“Here.” She pressed the penlight into his hand, feeling her control seeping back. Knowing she wasn’t alone had a steadying effect, and Noah’s staid calm was infectious. “I was just coming in. I started up the steps and found her.” She couldn’t keep her voice from shaking a little.

The penlight’s beam picked out the woman’s figure. It wasn’t just a nightmare, then.

Noah bent over the woman, touching her face as Joanna had done. Then he turned back, his strong body a featureless silhouette.

“Who is she?”

The question startled her. “I don’t know. I didn’t even think about it. I just wanted to get help. We must call the police and tell them to send paramedics, too.”

Not wasting time, Noah was already halfway out. “I’ll be back as soon as I’ve called. Yell if…” He let that trail off, but she understood. He’d be there if she needed him.

But she’d be fine. She was a grown woman, a businesswoman, not a skittish girl. Given all it had taken her to reach this point, she had to act the part.

Joanna settled as close to the woman as she could get on the narrow stairway. After a moment’s hesitation, she put her hand gently on the woman’s wrist. The pulse beat steadily under her touch, and Joanna’s fear subsided slightly. That was a good sign, wasn’t it?

The darkness and the silence grew oppressive, and she shivered. If only she had a blanket… She heard the thud of Noah’s hurrying footsteps. He stopped at the bottom of the stairs.

“They’re on their way. I’d best stay by the door so I can flag them down when they come. How is she?”

“No change.” Worry broke through the careful guard she’d been keeping. “What if she’s seriously injured? What if I’m to blame? She fell on my steps, after all.”

“Ach, Joanna, that’s foolishness.” Noah’s deep voice sounded firmly from the darkness. “It can’t be your fault, and most likely she’ll be fine in a day or two.”

Noah’s calm, steady voice was reassuring, and she didn’t need more light to know that his expression was as steady and calm as always.

“Does anything get under your guard?” she said, slightly annoyed that he could take the accident without apparent stress.

“Not if I can help it.” There might have been a thread of amusement in his voice. “It’s enough to worry about the poor woman’s recovery without imagining worse, ain’t so?”

“I suppose.” She straightened her back against the wall, reminding herself again that she was a grown woman, owner of her own business, able to cope with anything that came along.

But she didn’t feel all that confident right now. She felt worried. Whatever Noah might say, her instinct was telling her that this situation meant trouble. How and why, she didn’t know, but trouble nonetheless.

Don’t miss what happens next in
Amish Protector *by Marta Perry!*
Available April 2020 wherever HQN books and ebooks are sold.

HQNBooks.com

Copyright © 2020 by Martha P. Johnson

PHMPEXP0420

Get 4 FREE REWARDS!
We'll send you 2 FREE Books plus 2 FREE Mystery Gifts.
LOVE INSPIRED SUSPENSE
Trained To Defend
CHRISTY BARRITT
K-9 MOUNTAIN GUARDIANS
LARGER PRINT
LOVE INSPIRED SUSPENSE
Secret Mountain Hideout
TERRI REED
LARGER PRINT
Love Inspired Suspense books showcase how courage and optimism unite in stories of faith and love in the face of danger.
FREE Value Over $20
YES! Please send me 2 FREE Love Inspired Suspense novels and my 2 FREE mystery gifts (gifts are worth about $10 retail). After receiving them, if I don't wish to receive any more books, I can return the shipping statement marked "cancel." If I don't cancel, I will receive 6 brand-new novels every month and be billed just $5.24 each for the regular-print edition or $5.99 each for the larger-print edition in the U.S., or $5.74 each for the regular-print edition or $6.24 each for the larger-print edition in Canada. That's a savings of at least 13% off the cover price. It's quite a bargain! Shipping and handling is just 50¢ per book in the U.S. and $1.25 per book in Canada.* I understand that accepting the 2 free books and gifts places me under no obligation to buy anything. I can always return a shipment and cancel at any time. The free books and gifts are mine to keep no matter what I decide.
Choose one: ☐ Love Inspired Suspense Regular-Print (153/353 IDN GNWN)
☐ Love Inspired Suspense Larger-Print (107/307 IDN GNWN)
Name (please print)
Address
Apt. #
City
State/Province
Zip/Postal Code
Mail to the Reader Service:
IN U.S.A.: P.O. Box 1341, Buffalo, NY 14240-8531
IN CANADA: P.O. Box 603, Fort Erie, Ontario L2A 5X3
Want to try 2 free books from another series? Call 1-800-873-8635 or visit www.ReaderService.com.
*Terms and prices subject to change without notice. Prices do not include sales taxes, which will be charged (if applicable) based on your state or country of residence. Canadian residents will be charged applicable taxes. Offer not valid in Quebec. This offer is limited to one order per household. Books received may not be as shown. Not valid for current subscribers to Love Inspired Suspense books. All orders subject to approval. Credit or debit balances in a customer's account(s) may be offset by any other outstanding balance owed by or to the customer. Please allow 4 to 6 weeks for delivery. Offer available while quantities last.
Your Privacy—The Reader Service is committed to protecting your privacy. Our Privacy Policy is available online at www.ReaderService.com or upon request from the Reader Service. We make a portion of our mailing list available to reputable third parties that offer products we believe may interest you. If you prefer that we not exchange your name with third parties, or if you wish to clarify or modify your communication preferences, please visit us at www.ReaderService.com/consumerschoice or write to us at Reader Service Preference Service, P.O. Box 9062, Buffalo, NY 14240-9062. Include your complete name and address.
LIS20R

IF YOU ENJOYED THIS BOOK WE THINK YOU WILL ALSO LOVE

LOVE INSPIRED

INSPIRATIONAL ROMANCE

Uplifting stories of faith, forgiveness and hope.

Fall in love with stories where faith helps guide you through life's challenges, and discover the promise of a new beginning.

6 NEW BOOKS AVAILABLE EVERY MONTH!

LIXSERIES2020

LOVE INSPIRED

INSPIRATIONAL ROMANCE

UPLIFTING STORIES OF FAITH, FORGIVENESS AND HOPE.

Join our social communities to connect with other readers who share your love!

Sign up for the Love Inspired newsletter at **LoveInspired.com** to be the first to find out about upcoming titles, special promotions and exclusive content.

CONNECT WITH US AT:

Facebook.com/LoveInspiredBooks

Twitter.com/LoveInspiredBks

Facebook.com/groups/HarlequinConnection

LISOCIAL2020